Scandal on the Sand

The Barefoot Bay Series #3

roxanne st. claire

Critical Reviews of
Roxanne St. Claire Novels

"St. Claire, as always, brings a scorching tear-up-the-sheets romance combined with a great story: dealing with real issues starring memorable characters in vivid scenes."
— Romantic Times Magazine

"Non-stop action, sweet and sexy romance, lively characters, and a celebration of family and forgiveness."
— Publishers Weekly

"Plenty of heat, humor, and heart!"
— USA Today's Happy Ever After blog

"It's safe to say I will try any novel with St. Claire's name on it."
— www.smartbitchestrashybooks.com

"The writing was perfectly on point as always and the pace of the story was flawless. But be forewarned that you will laugh, cry, and sigh with happiness. I sure did."
— www.harlequinjunkies.com

"The Barefoot Bay series is an all-around knockout, soul-satisfying read. Roxanne St. Claire writes with warmth and heart and the community she's built at Barefoot Bay is one I want to visit again and again."
— Mariah Stewart, New York Times bestselling author

"This book stayed with me long after I put it down."
— All About Romance

THE
Barefoot Bay
SERIES

Welcome to Barefoot Bay! On these sun-washed shores you'll meet heroes who'll steal your heart, heroines who'll make you stand up and cheer, and characters who quickly become familiar and beloved. Some are spicy, some are sweet, but every book in the Barefoot Bay series stands alone, and tempts readers to come back again and again. So, kick off your shoes and fall in love with billionaires, brides, bodyguards, silver foxes, and more...all on one dreamy island.

Want to know the day the next Roxanne St. Claire book is released? Sign up for the newsletter! You'll get brief monthly e-mails about new releases and book sales.

http://www.roxannestclaire.com/newsletter.html

Scandal on the Sand

roxanne st. claire

Dedication

This book is dedicated to faithful reader, avid fan, and dear friend Ramona "Mona" Kekstadt who deserves her own umbrella on the sands of Barefoot Bay!

Chapter One

I t was her eyes. As soon as Nate caught a glimpse of the arresting color, somehow both impossibly ocean blue and bottle green, he had to talk to the woman, listening carefully as she was introduced to one of his friends.

"You remember Liza Lemanski, the great unraveler of red tape."

He didn't waste a second moving closer, getting a whiff of a barely-there citrus scent. "I like a woman who can unravel," he said with a wink.

"Good." When she turned to him, her turquoise gaze held no hint of playfulness. "Because I've come to do a little unraveling."

His friend made some kind of parting jab, reminding Nate that he was up third in the exhibition softball game that was about to start, but Nate's attention was on the beauty in front of him. "So, who's getting unraveled, blue eyes?" he asked.

"You."

Nice. "And I like a woman who doesn't mess around."

"That's not what I hear." She still wasn't smiling,

making him wonder if the comment was a flirt or not. "We need to talk, Mr. Ivory."

That would be...*not*. Did he know her and forget those gorgeous eyes? Anything was possible, of course. With him, everything was possible. Or used to be.

How long would his past mistakes haunt him? Was he about to get an earful of how he'd made promises he'd never kept or taken phone numbers he'd never used or...worse? It could always be worse. Instantly, he felt his protective privacy walls rise like titanium barriers as he automatically reached for the sunglasses in his pocket.

"Sure, sure, let's talk after the game." Slipping them on, he took all the humor out of his tone and a step in the other direction.

She came with him, shaking back some long dark hair to make sure he could see she meant business. "Let's talk now."

"It'll only be three innings and then we're having a cocktail party at sea. We can unravel anything you want." He lifted his hand in a halfhearted wave goodbye.

"I prefer *now*."

Damn. He glanced around the large beachfront deck where he had just finished the press conference announcing the plan to launch a minor-league baseball team in Barefoot Bay. But no one came to his rescue. His business partners were already headed toward the sand for the softball game they'd put together to cap off the media event.

"Sorry, I gotta run. I'm batting cleanup."

"Yes, you are. Right this minute. With me."

Pushy little thing, wasn't she? Protected by reflective lenses, he let his gaze drift over her, lingering on fine cheekbones and lush lips that hadn't yet given him a real smile. Farther down, things got even better, with generous cleavage peeking out of a V-neck T-shirt and a tiny waist and soft curves under her jeans. She couldn't be five-four and a hundred and ten soaking wet.

"What's this about?" he asked, getting a sense that it *wasn't* about seeing her soaking wet, either.

"I need your signature."

"Oh." Relief washed through him as he let out the breath he'd been holding since he heard the edge in her voice. "You want an autograph?"

"No, I want your *signature*."

He didn't like the sound of that. "Listen, sweetheart, I have to play a ball game. So, later's better." Later, he'd be surrounded by his rec softball team and some pro ballplayers, safe from any accusations, suggestions, or sob story she might fling at him.

"Over here." She gestured toward an empty table that the wait staff of the Casa Blanca Resort & Spa had already cleared. Everyone had disappeared to the beach to watch the game.

Which was where he suddenly wanted very much to be.

"Whatever it is, make it fast." He purposely took all tease from his tone. She was hot, no doubt about it, but for some reason he smelled big trouble in this little package.

She responded by scraping a chair over the wooden deck as she pulled it out...*for him*. He stayed where he was while she took the other chair and opened up a large handbag.

"Okay...Liza." He rolled the name on his tongue,

taking time to appreciate the sassy and sexy sound of it and wishing she were a little more of both.

"I really think you're going to want to be sitting down for this," she said.

"What do you have?" Irritation prickled his spine at her icy tone. Irritation and worry. He'd sworn on his life that there wouldn't be any more scandals, no more headlines, no more sexts that made their way to Perez Hilton's blog. Oh, that had been a bad week. The Colonel had *not* been amused.

She snapped a large manila envelope on the table.

"Pictures?" he guessed with a mirthless snort. "How original." Every stinking blackmailing female in a nightclub had their secret cell phone shots. Which was why he'd sworn off the club scene along with the rest of his far-too-active social life.

When she didn't answer, he ventured closer. "Oh, don't tell me, TMZ has offered five figures." He could only imagine what she had. "Let me guess. You've got 'Naughty Nate' bare-ass naked in Vegas or Cabo. He's got a joint in one hand and a fifth of Tito's in the other. Some dot-com billionaire's wife is grabbing his johnson, and they're about to fall into a hot tub with four more blondes."

Sickening that he could describe that situation a little too clearly. Swallowing a wave of self-loathing, he watched her slide a packet of papers onto the table, along with a spiral notebook.

What the—

"Nate! You're on deck!"

He ignored the announcement, hollered from the sand, instead dropping into the chair next to her.

"So, how much?" he demanded, a sixth sense already

telling him what was going down here. The question went against everything he'd been taught as a member of a family with the iconic—and ironic—last name of *Ivory*. A family that was anything but pure and had trained all members that the first check was just that…the *first*. A blackmailer never went away.

But he absolutely refused to get embroiled in one more public mess and, damn it, if he had to pay to get rid of her, he would. Whatever it took to prove that he was worthy of the family name and…the chance to see that dark disapproval erased from his grandfather's eyes.

"I don't want money," she finally said.

Then what? Access to the Hollywood studio his older brother ran? A meeting with his other brother, the senator? Maybe insider-trading information from his cousin on Wall Street?

"Everybody wants something, Liza," he said on a sigh. Especially from an Ivory.

For the first time, the closest thing to a sweet expression settled on her lovely features. Her lips finally relaxed into a hint of a smile. Dark brows unfurrowed, and a slight blush of pink deepened her creamy complexion.

"Yes, everybody does want something," she whispered. "And I want you to sign this document." She slid the paper toward him. "And then I will go away and you can play softball and drink in Cabo with other guys' wives and have cocktails *under* the sea, for all I care." She flattened him with a dead-eyed look. "Sign, and I promise you will never see or hear from me again."

He had to slide off his shades to read the paper, blinking at the legalese, his name typed neatly in the blanks. And…*Dylan Cassidy, age four.*

"Who's Dylan?"

"Your son."

The words slammed like a power-punch to his temple, and for a second he actually saw stars. A *kid?* He'd been so careful. His whole freaking adult life, he'd been so damn careful about this. Very slowly, he lifted his gaze from the page to her face, digging like a dog in dirt for a shred of a recollection of this woman, a date, a night, an encounter, a damn quickie in the back room of a party.

Nothing.

"I don't even remember you," he said, the words sounding as jagged as they felt. How wasted had he been to forget this girl?

"Of course you don't remember me," she said. "I've never met you."

"But...this..." He tried to focus on the paper again, but a slow fire of horror sparked in his gut and rolled up to burn his chest as the words stopped dancing in front of his eyes. *Voluntary Termination of Parental Rights.* "This isn't a paternity suit?"

"No, this is my guarantee that I can live in complete peace without an ax hanging over my head."

What the hell? "I'm confused. Do you mind explaining what you are talking about?"

"I want you to sign this so that I don't wake up some morning and find out the Ivory family is out to take Dylan away from me."

"You said he...we..." He let out a puff of pure frustration. "I don't get this at all. If I'm signing away rights to your child, how can I have never met you?"

"I'm not his mother." She nudged the paper closer. "Not that you care about her or have bothered to check,

6

but his mother is dead, and I'm his legal guardian. And all you need to do is sign right there, and I'll handle the rest of the red tape. As you heard, I'm good at that."

Dead? Was she saying this boy was an *orphan*? Another cascade of unfamiliar emotions squeezed some air out of his lungs, but he forced himself to breathe and get to the facts, starting with the obvious. "Who is his mother?"

Her expression was total surprise, followed by a resigned shrug. "I suppose more than one woman has told you she's pregnant in your lifetime. Her name was Carrie Cassidy."

Slowly, he shook his head to say he'd never heard that name in his life. "What happened to her?" Maybe that would jog his memory.

"She was in a car accident a year ago and died almost instantly." She held out a pen. "Please. Make it easy on all of us."

Easy? Nothing about this conversation was easy.

She leaned forward and speared him with her jewel-toned gaze. "She left enough details about how you dumped her, penniless and pregnant, to fill a whole issue of the *National Enquirer*. Imagine the headline: *Nathaniel Ivory, Deadbeat Baby Daddy*."

It didn't take much of an imagination to visualize how well that issue would sell.

She was right about one thing—signing would be easy. Two scratches of a pen and he could go play softball and drink scotch and live his life. No scandal, no problems, no...

No way.

"I'm not signing anything."

Close. She was so close that every cell in Liza's body was quivering, but somehow she managed to keep her cool. Finally facing Nathaniel Ivory, after eleven months of planning for this moment, she wasn't about to let him know that her insides were mush and her heart was exploding against her ribs and she could throw up from the nerves. She couldn't let him know how much this mattered or that she was totally bluffing about the *Enquirer* because…she wouldn't dream of dragging Dylan through mud like that.

She was doing this *for* Dylan, who was everything to her.

"What's in that notebook?" Nate asked, attempting to reach for it, but she snatched it away.

"No, you don't."

"I knew you were lying." He spat out the accusation with disgust.

"I'm not lying!" She clutched the book, holding it to her chest. "You could take this and run. I'm not letting you have it."

"Run? Run where? To the beach? Who *is* this dead woman and what fiction did she write in that book? What proof do you have? Have you ever heard of DNA testing? Do you really think I'm going to sign something without answers? You think I can't smell the stink of your scam from a mile away?" The questions came at her like bullets from an automatic rifle, each one lodging in her throat and chest and gut. "Forget the pretend mother and bogus baby, what is *your* deal, Liza Lemanski?"

Oh, she'd been so close. She saw the moment he'd wavered and nearly signed the document. Almost but not quite there…like everything in her life. And now he thought she was a con artist. Great.

"My deal is that you sign this paper." *Stay on point, Liza. Don't let him sway you.*

"Why now?" he asked. "Didn't you say she died a year ago? And this alleged son is four? What took so long to collect your cash, huh?"

"I'm not…" She shook her head. "You told her you wouldn't help her, and I didn't know you were the father until she died and left me as his guardian. I'm not scared of you or your family like she was." A white lie, but she had to appear strong. "I want a clean slate as I start the formal adoption process, so, please"—she tapped the paper—"let me have that and that will be the end of this."

"And you come up to me at the end of a press conference and throw this at me?"

"I read in the local paper that you'd be here this morning and I…" Called in sick, grabbed the papers she already had prepared—working in the County Clerk's office did have its advantages—and put her plan into action.

"Why not approach my lawyer? That's how things like this are done."

"I thought it would be—"

"Easier to extort money."

"I don't *want* money." She fisted her hand, punching the air. "And I know you don't want a child."

"How do you know anything about me?"

Holding the brightly colored spiral notebook, she picked at the half-peeled $3.99 Ross price tag on the back. "It's all in here, your name, your description, your words to her. But when you read all that, I have to be sure this book is protected. It's all I have to prove my case."

"Then maybe you don't have much of a case."

"Oh, I have a case. And I have a child who…" *Looks a hell of a lot like you.* "Who I want to keep, without living in fear that someone is going to try to claim him."

"So you've said." He inched forward. A lock of chestnut hair fell over his brow, close to the golden-brown eyes that looked so much like…like Dylan's. "What do you *really* want, honey, because I don't believe a word you're saying."

Tiny beads of perspiration stung at her neck and temples, her cool slipping with each second that she had to face him. "I want that child. I want him safe and protected with me."

Something flickered in his eyes, a flash that went by so fast she wasn't positive she'd seen it, but she knew she'd hit some kind of emotional hot button.

"And you don't," she added, because what if *that* was the hot button she'd hit? What if he wanted a child? "It says so right here." She tapped Carrie's journal, maybe a little harder than necessary. "It says a lot of things about you that I don't think you want out in public."

Hollow threat, of course, but still she threw that trump card down again, hoping it would work. Surely a man with his lifestyle, money, and famously documented inability to commit didn't want a child he'd fathered almost five years ago.

Did he?

"Hey, Nate!"

Startled at the man's voice, Liza turned to see Zeke

Nicholas, one of the other men who'd been involved in the announcement today, jogging across the patio deck, impatience darkening his expression. "You missed your at bat, man. Come on!"

Nate held up his hand and shook his head.

"'Scuse me," Zeke said to Liza as he reached the table. "But I have to steal this heartthrob for just a—"

"Shut it, Zeke!" Fury sparked in Nate's eyes, but he didn't take them off Liza, making her certain his anger was not directed at his friend.

Zeke froze midstep. "Everything okay here?"

"We're fine," Liza said, seizing the opportunity. "I'm getting Mr. Ivory's autograph." Not that she had any real hope left that he'd sign, but maybe with his friend here, he'd buckle. It was worth a shot. "Right here, sir. And then you'll make the second inning."

His nostrils flared as he took a slow breath and shook his head. "You have to play without me, Zeke." Suddenly, he stood, gathering up the papers and the envelope in one swooping motion. "Liza and I are going somewhere more private."

She didn't move but glanced at Zeke, who seemed as surprised as Liza was. "So we should meet you on board the yacht later, for cocktails?"

Nate shook his head. "Sorry, the party's canceled. Come on, Liza." He reached for her hand, and when she didn't take his, he closed his fingers over her wrist to gently pull her up. "I can't wait one more minute to get you alone."

Zeke looked skyward. "So much for 'the new Nate.'"

"Go play softball," he said through clenched teeth. "I've got something more important to deal with."

With a stiff nod, Zeke left, but Liza held her ground. "I'm not going anywhere with you."

"We're not talking about this here, out in the open with staff running around. Any one of them could be recording this conversation on a cell phone."

She glanced at the busboy who openly stared at Nate as he slowed purposely by their table. He was right, of course. Everyone was interested in his business.

"Look." He leaned closer, the low tenor of his voice practically vibrating the air between them. "I don't know you or this kid or this Carrie character from Adam. But if you think I'm putting my name on anything without details and dates, along with legal, scientific, and medical proof, you're out of your mind. Let's go."

She pressed the notebook to her heart, a flimsy four-dollar shield against his billion-dollar onslaught. "I have all that. And there's no doubt of paternity."

He tried to usher her away from the table. "Oh, there's plenty of doubt. I'm not stupid, and I don't make mistakes when I mess around with strangers."

"You're calling her a stranger? Your lover for almost two months until you found out she was pregnant and dumped her?"

His eyes widened, then he shook his head with a soft, sarcastic laugh. "I've heard some pretty creative scams, honey, really, I have. But I gotta hand it to you. This is good. Innovative, complex, and ballsy." He had the nerve to give her a salacious grin and openly check her out from head to toe, sending a completely unwanted awareness through her. "And all wrapped up in a hot little package with sex-kitten eyes and my kind of rack. It's good, kid. It's good."

Sex kitten? Kid? His kind of *rack*?

What had Carrie been thinking when she fell for this tool? "Nothing about this is innovative or ballsy and, honestly, the story isn't that complex. Let me spell it out for you."

"Not here."

"Right here, and right now."

Another waiter walked by, slowing his steps, and glancing in their direction.

"Okay, okay," she finally gave in, walking with him off the deck to the beach, to the opposite side of where the game was being played. When they were completely out of earshot of anyone else, she took a breath of salt-infused air, mustering up momentum for her power-plea. But her sandals sank into soft sand, giving him even more of a height advantage.

She refused to cower.

"Listen to me," she said. "You can deny this all you want or pretend you never heard of her or claim you're too smart to make a mistake. But the facts are simple: Carrie had your child after you made it perfectly clear you wanted no part of a baby, and she spent three years in fear that you'd find her and claim him. She lived with me since she arrived in Florida, pregnant and unemployed, and became my best friend. She was killed by a drunk driver on I-75 a year ago and left me guardianship of her child, whom I plan to legally adopt and raise. I can't do that until I know for sure and certain you will never try to take him away from me. What's *ballsy* about that?"

"Where does the money come in?" he asked with no hesitation.

"I don't *want* money," she repeated on an exasperated sigh. Was that so hard for him to understand? "I want freedom and peace of mind and my…this…Dylan." She swallowed as she said his name. "I want Dylan." Safe, close, happy. That's what she wanted. "Honestly, that's all I've ever wanted since the day a cop showed up at my door and told me Carrie was dead."

He had the decency to at least feign sympathy. "Sorry, but…" He reached for the notebook, tugging it from her fingers. "Let me see that. Let me—"

Something slipped out of the pages, fluttering to the sand. He stooped down and snagged it as she did the same, their heads tapping lightly. He got the picture before she did, but Liza had a second to see it was the photo of Dylan she'd slipped into the back of the journal.

She reached for it, instantly protective, even of his photo. "That's—"

"Me," he finished, staring at it, still crouched down.

"No, I took that…" Her voice faded as she realized what he was saying. "Yeah, he looks like you. So much for an innovative and complex scam for money, huh?"

Staring at the photo, he let his backside drop onto the sand to sit. "He's an Ivory," he whispered, awe and disbelief and recognition making his voice thick.

She plopped down next to him. "What do you think I've been trying to tell you?"

"That changes everything."

Her heart plummeted. "How?"

"I have to…" He struggled with the words, and her brain raced to fill in the blank. Meet him? Take him? Claim him? What did he have to do now that he didn't want to do years ago when Carrie told him she was pregnant?

He exhaled. "I have to see that journal. Somewhere completely private."

"We can walk on the beach."

He shook his head and pointed his thumb at the baseball game behind him. "They'll come after me. Where do you live?"

"Too far and…" She didn't want him there. "No, let's go inside and sit at a table or in the lobby."

He gave her a funny look, slowly shaking his head as he stood, still looking at the picture. "You don't understand. I can't do that. People know me. They take pictures. They approach me. Let's just…" He gestured for her to follow him. "I have an idea."

But she didn't move, looking up at him, feeling so small and helpless and frustrated and scared. "Are you going to take him from me?" she managed to ask.

He reached down and took her hand, his silence almost worse than if he'd said yes.

Chapter Two

B lackmail would have been better, Nate thought as he maneuvered his Aston Martin through the narrow streets of Mimosa Key, headed for the harbor where he had a shot at relative privacy. She'd agreed to come along, clinging to her precious notebook.

Blackmail he could handle. The family was used to that sort of thing. But a four-year-old child whose mother—with a name he'd never heard in his life—was dead and left nothing but a journal? This was big. This was problematic. This was life-changing, and not in the way he wanted his life to change.

But...

He's an Ivory.

The family sure had some powerful, unstoppable genes, and Nate had spent enough time with cousins to know an Ivory when he saw an Ivory. And mistakes happen, obviously, so nothing was impossible.

But no one told him! He never left anyone *penniless* and *pregnant*.

A sensation he couldn't name, didn't understand, and already hated welled up in him. A bunch of them, to be fair. Anger, fear, frustration, and disbelief coiled around his gut. What if he had *inadvertently* done something like that? What if this claim was real?

Next to him, Liza had situated herself as close to the opposite side of the sports car as she could be without actually riding outside. Silent, she stared straight ahead, gnawing her lower lip and clutching that cheap notebook like it was the crown jewels.

Well, in some ways, it was. Maybe it held information that could get her a lot of money. That had to be her game, with the strategy of acting like it wasn't. Hell, at this point, he *hoped* that was her game, despite her vehement denials.

He'd far prefer a little friendly extortion to *fatherhood.*

Who was this woman claiming to have had a relationship with him? He broke the silence after about five minutes. "Carrie…Cassidy, did you say?"

"Her real name was Careen. Does that help?"

Not a bit. "I have absolutely no recollection of meeting a woman named Carrie or Careen or Cassidy, let alone sleeping with her. Let alone spending *months* with her. I don't spend months with my best friends, let alone…women."

"So I've heard. And read."

He slid her another look, trying to see past the intriguing eyes and waves of thick, dark hair to the villainess underneath. But all he saw was a great-looking woman chewing a hole in her lower lip, her arms wrapped around her chest protectively, popping some luscious cleavage out of her T-shirt.

He returned his attention to the road. He would not be diving into that particular weakness of his anytime soon. "So tell me everything about this so-called Carrie."

She let go of that lower lip, whipping around, eyes flashing like the Sri Lankan green sapphires that decorated the backsplash of his master bath.

"So-called?" She flung the words back at him. "Carrie Cassidy was a living, breathing, lovely young woman who died far too young. And she's the mother of your child, so show some respect, for God's sake."

"All right, all right." Once again, he rooted around his memory banks, many of those vaults pickled by substances he'd recently sworn off. "Where'd I meet her? When and how?"

"In Key West, about five years ago."

Five years ago he'd been twenty-five, living off a generous trust fund, ridiculously wild, a bona fide jet-setter who went from party to party on any continent, with any socialite, without a moment's concern about tomorrow. He did not, however, stick his dick *anywhere* without a condom. He might be reckless, but he wasn't dumb, and he'd heard enough lectures from brothers and cousins.

So, had he been in Key West that year? That was possible, even probable. He went there on a regular basis. Had he had sex with a girl there? Likely enough. But hadn't she said something about being with her for months?

"So, she claims we dated for two months?" he asked as he turned into the harbor parking lot.

"You were lovers," she corrected. "And there's no 'claiming' involved."

Definitely a lie. "I can guarantee you if I was hanging out with someone that long term, I'd remember."

She made a grunt of disgust.

"What? I'm being honest."

18

"Listen to yourself. Two months is a long-term relationship, and calling what you did with Carrie 'hanging out' sounds so..." She closed her eyes and shook her head, unable to come up with something awful enough to describe him.

So he helped. "Cavalier? Uncommitted? Casual? Apathetic? Detached? I've heard them all, my dear, and every single one is true."

"Have you heard 'asshole,' too?"

He bit back a chuckle. "What do you think?"

"I think..." She turned away and looked out the window as he slid the car into a parking spot. "I hope none of those things are hereditary."

The sadness in her voice did something to his insides that he didn't like at all. He chose to ignore it. "Don't count on it," he said. "Those traits are stamped into the Ivory DNA."

"Or you're raised that way."

"Hard to say," he agreed.

"Which is exactly why I don't want Dylan raised like that. I don't want him part of that greedy, egomaniacal, power-hungry clan."

Her words shot a jolt of defensiveness up his spine. He turned off the car, flipped his belt, and reached for the door handle. Before he opened it, he flattened her with a look to underscore the warning he was about to give.

"Here's the rule, Liza. I can insult my family, but no one else can." Without waiting for her response, he opened the door and stepped into the February sunshine, which was plenty warm this far south. Instantly, she popped up on the other side.

"Well, here's *my* rule: I don't want Dylan to be, what

19

was it you called yourself? Apathetic and cavalier and isolated?"

"I said *detached*. I'm not isolated."

She glanced around. "Then why are we here?"

"My boat is private." And isolated. He started walking toward the last slip, where he'd docked. Liza had to hurry to catch up, shouldering her bag. He reached the twenty-eight-foot cabin cruiser, and when he turned to offer her a hand, he found her eyeing the boat suspiciously.

"I'd hardly call this a yacht."

"Neither would I," he agreed, purposely saying no more as he helped her on board and then unlocked the doors to the lounge inside.

"Can't we sit out here?" she asked, pointing to the leather sofas and captain's chairs on the deck.

He shrugged, though it was more comfortable inside with the living room and bar. But he felt relatively alone and safe, since very few people knew he'd rented this slip, so he sat across from her and reached out his hand.

"Give me that journal, please."

She looked back at him. "Are you going to throw it overboard?"

"No."

"Promise?"

"I swear, and my word is good."

Even in the sunlight, he could see the color wash from her face, and very slowly, she took out the maroon and pink notebook. He opened the cover, and the first thing he saw was another picture, this one of a woman holding a baby. Blond, blue-eyed, with pixie-like features and a sunny smile.

"That's Carrie, right after Dylan was born." She

stood near him—maybe planning to dive in if he tossed the book—looking at the same picture.

He studied the woman's features, angling the photo so he could get every detail. And then something clicked. Something cleared. Something snapped into place like a puzzle piece.

Carrie? "No, not Carrie," he said, peering at her face, digging through a faded memory. "Her name is…" He closed his eyes, pulling the moment from the past. Yes, it was Key West. It was crazy. It was… "Bailey."

Liza lowered herself to the bench to sit next to him. "No, her name is not Bailey."

"Bailey Banks. I remember because she said she was named after a jewelry store, and I looked it up after…after…" After they had sex in the back of a limo. Fast, furious, forgettable sex. "I wanted to find her again, but I…" He shook his head, remembering the real frustration at the time. "No one knew her. I tried to find her. I asked around, but no one had ever seen her before. She must have crashed the party, and the number she gave me was bogus. I never heard from her again, and I wanted to."

And not because she was a good time. Not at all. Bailey Banks had been camera-happy, and that had scared the shit out of Nate, even back then before Instagram and Twitter. Right before she slipped out of the limo, she laughingly waved her camera and told him she'd had a video running the whole time.

So I never forget this night with Naughty Nate! Her parting shot was crystal clear in his vodka-soaked memory.

The next day, sober enough to be scared spitless, he went searching for the woman and her camera, but came up empty-handed on both. Eventually, he'd forgotten she existed, and no videos ever surfaced.

"That's not her version of the events at all." Liza gestured to the notebook. "You better read that."

"Are there more, um, pictures of her?" Or *him*?

"I have a few at home. Pictures I took."

"But no others? No pictures or…anything?"

She shook her head, and he took another look at the photo, everything from that night coming back to him, decadent moment by decadent moment. Bailey Banks. She'd been easy, sexy, and more than a little starstruck. And, of course, he'd taken advantage of that.

Self-loathing rose like bile, but he tamped it down. He was better now, different, and on the right road.

Wasn't he?

"I remember some of her story," he said. "She told me she ran away from home at fifteen."

Liza looked at him like he had two heads. "She didn't run away at fifteen. She was raised in Arizona, an only child, and close to her parents, who, as you know, because you *went to their funeral,* died in a fire.*"

What the *hell*? "Someone is on crack," he said. "You or her. But I never went to anyone's funeral in Arizona."

"Read the notebook," she finally said, pushing up from the bench.

He didn't answer, but something was not right. Something was so not right with this picture. Nate leaned back and turned the page, to the picture of a boy who could have been him twenty-five years ago. "Let's see what we've got here."

Other than a big, fat mess.

Liza knew every word in that book. Every turn of phrase, every scrawled sentence, every gut-wrenching emotion that spilled out like Carrie's tears, every time she mentioned Nathaniel Ivory's name. The account of a naïve and innocent girl's relationship with a rich, famous, heartless bastard wasn't very long, maybe fifteen handwritten pages, but it made for good reading.

If you like fantasies with unhappy endings.

While he read, Liza walked around the deck of the boat, trying not to watch him, and failing a few times. She heard the pages flip, quickly, so she occasionally turned to catch a glimpse of him, bent over the notebook.

Any other time, any other circumstance, and she'd react like, well, like any other woman. He was easily six-one or six-two, with strong, square shoulders and the kind of chest a woman wanted to...rest against. Or explore with two hands. His face was classically handsome, with thick brows and a Roman nose, and a hint of shadow where his whiskers grew.

Easy wit, a sexy smile, and dark topaz eyes all attracted her more than she wanted to admit. But attraction wasn't an option...she needed that signature and then, just as she said, she never wanted to see him again.

He flipped the next page harder than the time before.

Did the truth make him angry? Unless...Carrie had lied.

No. Impossible. Carrie was sweet, simple, kind, loving, and guileless. The day she'd walked into Liza's cubicle at the County Clerk's office to apply for a job, the young woman nearly collapsed, whispering her secret that she was broke and expecting. And Liza had instantly liked her and soon loved her like the sister she never had.

In the following three and a half years, Carrie had never once revealed who Dylan's father was, except to say his family was powerful enough to scare her. But after she died, Liza found the notebook and finally understood just how powerful that family was. Her friend's secrecy and fears made complete sense.

According to what she wrote, Carrie worried that Nate would find her and change his mind about the baby. The journal filled in some holes and confirmed the hints that Carrie had dropped all along.

Right? Or had Carrie made the whole thing up?

"I don't know what to believe anymore," Liza whispered to herself as she stepped into the lounge area of the boat. Which was as visually stunning as the golden-eyed god who owned it.

Every piece of furniture and decor was a different shade of cream, covered in leather, suede, or marble, with masculine touches of gleaming teak. No surprise, money oozed from every corner, a testament to the famous Ivory family fortune.

He seemed to think money was all she wanted. Well, it would be nice if he wanted to throw a thousand into a college fund for Dylan, sure. But what she wanted— freedom from worry—was priceless.

"I read it."

She turned to find him standing in the glass sliders that separated the deck from the lounge, an unreadable emotion etched on his strong cheekbones and square jaw. Unless *ice cold* was an emotion, then she could read it just fine.

"This is complete and utter fiction. You know that, don't you? Pure fabrication."

Right now, she didn't know anything. "You said you recognized her when you saw her picture. You met in Key West. You...you had...you slept with her, didn't you?"

He huffed a soft breath and dropped onto one of the creamy sofas, tossing the notebook next to him. Liza stayed standing.

"Here's what's true," he said. "And I'm happy to swear on a stack of Bibles or in a court of law or whatever you want me to do that will make this legit."

What she wanted to "make this legit" was for him to sign and disappear forever. Both possibilities were becoming more remote with each passing minute. "Just be honest," she said. "And tell me your side of the story."

He nodded a few times, gathering his thoughts. "If your Carrie and this girl I recognize as Bailey are really the same person?" With his left hand, he flipped the cover of the book, opening to her picture. "I think they are. So, then about three paragraphs of this is true. I met her at a party, exactly as it says here, in the driveway of a beach house a friend of mine owns. She thought I was the valet, and I let her think that for a few minutes. It was funny, we flirted, exactly like she said. A few minutes later, she saw me inside and we had a good laugh, exactly like she said. We had a few drinks and talked, exactly like she said."

"She called it love at first sight."

He closed his eyes. "I would categorize it as mutual

attraction that led to lust. Nothing remotely like love took place."

Assuming a man like him even knew what love was. "And you took her home and were with her when she got the call about her parents that night, right?"

Very slowly, he shook his head. "That's not what happened."

She waited, crossing her arms and leaning against the bar.

"I did take her home. At least, I had my limo drop her off after we..." He swallowed, hard, then met Liza's gaze. "We, uh, got intimate in the back of the limo."

She lifted a brow. "Intimate?"

"We had sex," he said bluntly. "Wholly consensual, lightning-fast, and utterly meaningless sex."

Each word was like a hammer striking a nail into her heart. Was that how Dylan was conceived? That certainly wasn't Carrie's story.

"I dropped her off at an apartment building, but she wouldn't even let me walk her to the door," he continued. "She gave me her number and disappeared." A new kind of pain etched across his handsome features. "I swear to God I tried to find her, and it was like she was vapor. Bogus number, didn't live in that apartment, didn't know anyone at the party. She was gone." He cleared his throat and continued. "So that part she wrote about the phone call from the fire department in Tucson? Fiction. At least, it wasn't *me* with her that night, holding her, arranging for a private plane to get her home. Never happened."

Of all the possible responses she'd played out in her mind, Liza never expected this. Never expected the journal to be a half-truth.

"The trip to France?" she asked. "The vacation with your family? The two weeks at your place in Hawaii? The hot-air balloon ride when you said you loved her?"

With each question, his head slowly moved from side to side. "Never happened."

Her legs couldn't hold her anymore, so Liza finally eased into the closest chair, sinking into the buttery leather with a barely audible sigh. "Are you saying that whole whirlwind affair was a...lie?"

"That account of our relationship in that notebook is a story, a fabrication, a complete work of fiction," he said carefully. "Yes, I think I know this woman and, yes, we had sex. With a condom," he added. "What did she tell you?"

"She never..." She cleared her throat, having a feeling this wasn't going to get her the signature she needed and wanted. "She never actually told me your name."

It was his turn to stare in disbelief. "So you're basing this entire thing on some teenager's attempt at a bad romance novel? A woman who has, as far as we know, at least two names."

"She wasn't a teenager." But she wasn't much more than that. "I saw her legal document, and I know her name was Careen Cassidy. And Dylan looks like you."

He lifted a shoulder and nodded. "I'll give you that. But it could be a coincidence."

"And you did have sex with her."

"I had sex with a girl who had a different name and looks a little like that one in the picture." He leaned forward. "How well do you know this Carrie person?"

Ire shot through her. *This Carrie person* had been

dear to her. "Well. Very well. We lived together, and I was in the hospital room when Dylan was born, and I've helped raise him."

"How did you meet her?"

"She applied for a job at the County Clerk's office when I worked in personnel, and we hit it off in the interview." Carrie's sob story had ripped Liza's heart out, and she'd invited the poor girl to stay with her until she found an apartment...and she'd never left. "We became really good friends and, well, she needed help and—"

"But not such good friends that she'd tell you who fathered the baby?"

The truth jabbed at her. "She told me you—he—had made it clear you didn't want anything to do with the baby, and she'd rather forget about you."

His eyes flashed. "I never told anyone anything like that, because we never had another conversation after I dropped her off at an apartment complex that night," he insisted, his voice rising with impatience. "She made it all up."

Was that possible? Inside, way down low in her belly, Liza grew cold and afraid. Had she been such a pushover that Carrie lied from day one? She'd always had a soft spot for strays, and she had the four cats to prove it. But everyone who met Carrie loved her, even Liza's mother, who didn't usually love anyone if they didn't have access to the right country club.

"What about the notebook?" he asked. "Where did it come from?"

"I found it hidden in her belongings after she died. When I read it, I realized just how rich and powerful a family she'd meant when I saw the name Ivory."

"And it didn't occur to you that this whole story was a product of her imagination?"

She shook her head, feeling incredibly vulnerable and foolish. "What occurred to me was that, if I could find you, I could get you to sign a TPR, er, a Termination of Parental Rights waiver, which is what I had urged her to do all along. I work with legal documents every day. I know they carry tremendous weight in court, and if you don't have them in order, it could come back to haunt you."

He didn't answer for a moment, his gaze on the picture that faced up. "Was she drunk?"

Liza blinked at him, the question throwing her. "Excuse me?"

"When she died. You said it was an accident on the highway. Was she drunk?"

She almost laughed. "I never saw Carrie drink anything stronger than iced tea. She was insanely healthy and, for your information, she never even went on a date in the time we were roommates. I tried to fix her up with a friend once, and she refused. She said Dylan was her only man."

That indiscernible flicker of emotion passed over his face again. He looked down, bracing his elbows on his knees to rest his chin on tight fists. "And what about Dylan?"

Her heart rate rose at the question. The tenderness in the tone scared her. "What about him?"

"How is he? His mom is dead and, well, he's an orphan."

"Not technically, since I—"

"No, I guess if he has a father, he's not an orphan."

She tried to swallow, but her mouth was dry and

tasted metallic. Fear. She was tasting real, live terror that she could lose Dylan. Why in the hell hadn't she left well enough alone? This was exactly what Carrie feared. He'd have never come after Dylan, and now...

"How is he?" he asked again.

"What do you mean? He's..." Perfect. Adorable. Sweet as candy and as good as gold. But something in her kept her from sharing. What if Nate fell in love with Dylan, too? And how could he not? Everyone fell in love with Dylan at first sight. "He's fine."

"Is he well-adjusted? Healthy? Normal? Smart? Going to school? Reading yet?"

She would have laughed at how much like a dad he sounded except...nothing about that was funny. He *was* Dylan's dad and, as such, had some rights. Not legal guardianship. She did have that. But, still, he had a right to know about his son.

She nodded. "Very healthy, very well-adjusted, crazy smart, and slightly temperamental. He's only four, so he doesn't read very many words yet, but he can spell." She laughed softly. "Oh, boy, he likes to spell." She smiled, thinking of the light in his eyes when she handed him a new pack of Matchbox cars last night. "He loves cars. Anything with wheels, actually."

"I was that way, too."

"Well, he's nothing like you." The words popped out, unfiltered, earning her a dark look. "I mean, well—"

"You don't know me."

Shrugging, she chose her words carefully. "In trying to find you and decide what to do about this situation, I read a lot about you, so—"

"Like I said, you don't *know* me."

"I know what your lifestyle is. I know you live on

30

boats and have a dozen houses and go to parties in Monte Carlo and don't have a real job."

"I wouldn't call sitting on four *Fortune* 500 corporate boards, managing two charitable foundations, and handling a few billion dollars' worth of investments 'unemployed.'"

"I wouldn't call your lifestyle stable."

He made a guttural sound of disgust, pushing himself to a stand so he loomed over her. "A lifestyle is not a person. A lifestyle is a word the media made up. A lifestyle—" He turned and paced across the room, stopping to put his hands on the bar as if he actually needed support. "I am so sick of this conversation."

She drew back in surprise. "Excuse me?"

"Not with you. But, I've had it with…others." Keeping his back to her and his face down, he let his shoulders rise and fall with a silent sigh. "When can I meet him?"

"Why…*what*?" Her heart faltered. "Meet Dylan? You can't *meet* him."

Very slowly, he turned, and she nearly startled from the ragged emotion on his face. She couldn't quite decipher what he was feeling, but it was powerful and personal. "I have every right to meet this child you claim is my son."

"For what reason?"

He gave her a look of disbelief. "To determine if he's really mine."

"No, no, that's not necessary."

He narrowed his eyes and moved imperceptibly closer. "Just what are you hiding, Liza Lemanski?"

"Nothing! I'm not hiding anything. Look." Fighting a

little wave of panic, she grabbed the bag she'd dropped on the table, flipping it open. "You don't have to meet him." If he met Dylan, he'd love Dylan. It was impossible not to. And then…he'd want to take Dylan. Just as Carrie feared.

"I have this. This is…" Her fingers closed around the small plastic box that she'd received from the lab. "This swab is a sample of his DNA. And these papers verify it's his, from my doctor. You can have it tested and compared to yours."

She put the box and a white envelope on the table.

"Why would I do that?"

"So you know I'm not lying."

"And then can I meet him?"

She looked up at him, swallowing hard, her whole body feeling like she was trying to turn a tide, and she'd never even expected this particular tsunami. "I really never thought you'd have any interest in meeting him," she said.

"Well, I do. Right now, as a matter of fact."

No, no, she would not let that happen. She gestured toward the DNA. "Just do the test and then…" *Sign the papers.* "Look, Nate, you don't want a child and you know it. How could you raise him? How would you guide him in life? When would you spend time with him? He needs parenting and I'm…I'm not his mother, but I love him dearly and deeply and the…the 'lifestyle' I'm giving him is normal, safe, and sane. I know I don't have a lot of money, but I give him love and attention and…" Damn it, her voice cracked. "Please don't use your family power to take my little boy." She stood up, driven by the need to plead and beg. Whatever it took to keep Dylan. "Please?"

32

For what seemed like an eternity, he didn't answer. But his gaze slipped to the box and swab she'd left on the table. "I'll think about it."

Right now, that was all she could ask.

Chapter Three

After a sleepless night, Nate texted Elliott Becker and they made plans to meet at the resort for an early run on the beach. When Nate jogged onto the hard-packed sand, he found Becker stretching, along with Zeke Nicholas, and neither one of them looked too happy with him.

"What the hell happened to you yesterday?" Zeke demanded.

"You wouldn't believe it if I told you," he said, though he'd already decided to confide in his friends. They were trustworthy and smart, plus they knew his family situation well enough to appreciate the magnitude of the problem.

"Some hot chick shows up and you disappear," Zeke said.

"Like you two haven't been MIA since you met Mandy and Frankie," Nate shot back, easing into a slow stretch to prepare for their run.

"We didn't ditch the game to get laid." Becker shook out his legs and started a slow jog.

If only he had, Nate thought. That would be so much easier to explain and so much more in character. Except, he wasn't that guy anymore.

"So who is this girl, Nate?" Zeke asked. "I saw her talking to Frankie at the end of the press conference, but no one else knew her."

Becker elbowed him. "Bet Nate knows her now. What bed did you leave her in this morning?"

"She's at home with"—*my son*—"a little boy."

Zeke threw him a surprised look. "She has a kid?"

"Long story." And Nate wasn't ready to delve into it all yet. Instead, he let his sneakers hit the sand near the water and picked up the pace. With his eye on the horizon, he let the morning sun warm his muscles.

"Better watch your step, Mr. Ivory," Becker said, slowing down to get next to Nate. "Zeke and I were just saying there's something dangerous to bachelors in the air down here."

Yeah, *fatherhood*. That was dangerous to bachelors. "Looks like it, the way you two fell like a couple of horny high schoolers," Nate shot back.

Unaffected, Becker and Zeke shared a grin, then looked at Nate like he was the one who'd done something stupid. In a moment, the three of them fell silent long enough to pick up the pace, run to the north end of the bay, turn around and get serious.

"Loser buys breakfast," Zeke said.

"Screw that," Becker said. "Loser buys the restaurant."

Zeke and Nate cracked up, but Becker didn't wait to hear them laugh at his joke, kicking sand as he sprinted away. Zeke swore under his breath and did the same thing, leaving Nate twenty feet behind them both in less than a few seconds.

Automatically, he took off, the wind whistling in his

ears. But he didn't have it today, watching both of them get way ahead.

Thoughts of his fitful night before rose up and wrecked his speed like they'd wrecked his sleep. Damn, he had to solve this problem or it would wreck his work, too. And he had too much riding on this new stadium project his friends had entrusted him to run to risk having something like this steal his attention.

Still, did he have a son? What did that mean to his life? Could he walk away from that boy? Should he?

And, of course, the eternal question: What would the Colonel do?

As if there could be a question. Nothing, absolutely nothing, mattered more to the Colonel than family. They were, as the old veteran liked to say, his secret weapon in the war of life. Nate knew how his grandfather would act at the possibility of the Ivory DNA floating in anyone's bloodstream: *Claim that child. He's one of ours.*

But how could he? Nate had just begun to get his act together, and, now…this. Nate had jumped on the chance to own and manage a minor-league team, and not just because no one else in the Ivory dynasty had their hands in professional baseball yet. He had to prove himself to his grandfather, and this was his best, and last, chance.

And now, another potential scandal that would be eaten up by the media could devour his shot at the respectability he knew the Colonel wanted to see. Unless Nate walked away quietly…but would that move make the Colonel proud? A man who put family above everything else?

Lost in thought, he barely heard Zeke call to him.

When Nate caught up with his friends, Becker was bent over, hands on his knees, a little winded but victorious. He looked up and caught his breath with a grin.

"Must have been quite a night for you, Ivory. I've never seen you lose a race."

"Or anything," Zeke added, eyeing him carefully. "What's wrong?"

"What's *right* is a better question. Let's eat, and I'll tell you."

A half hour later, at their favorite veranda table overlooking the beach, the three of them were still virtually alone in the beach deck of the resort restaurant. Comfortable that they had privacy, Nate told them everything and answered the questions he could.

"I hate to say this, especially because Frankie knows this woman, but I think it's a scam," Becker said, leaning back on the chair's back legs and crossing his arms. "She smells cash."

"But the kid looks like you?" Zeke asked. "Are you sure?"

"Freakishly," Nate confirmed. "And I definitely remember meeting the girl whose picture Liza showed me. And I happened to check the ship log last night, and sure enough, we were docked in Key West in April five years ago."

Zeke leaned forward. "If you got her pregnant in April, she'd have had a baby in January."

"Of course Einstein knows that," Becker joked.

Zeke ignored it, focused on Nate, always ready to use logic and math to solve a problem. "When's this kid's birthday?"

"I don't know, but he's four."

"He would have had to have turned four last month if

you have any possibility of being the father. Find out his birthday, and if the math works, get a test and…"

"And then start writing big checks," Becker said.

"I told you she doesn't want money."

Becker snorted.

"Hey, Frankie didn't want your multimillion-dollar offer for her land," Nate shot back, not sure why he felt the need to defend Liza, but he did.

"Because she's a Niner in her own right," Becker replied, referring not only to the name of their rec softball team in New York, but also the qualification to be on it: nine zeroes in each player's net worth. "Your little friend is a secretary in the County Clerk's office living with a kid whose alleged 'mother' is dead." He air-quoted to make his point, leaning closer as he gathered steam. "And she has some notebook with a fake story in it—"

"The beginning was true enough."

Becker waved that off. "Maybe she *was* friends with some chick you nailed five years ago, and that girl died and Liza dreamed up this whole thing. She has access to all this legal shit. She's probably figured out a con. Hey, it happens. It happened to Frankie's grandfather."

Nate had to nod. His family name was a golden ticket to some people who tried to swindle money.

"So, what's your plan?" Zeke asked. "How did you leave it?"

"She gave me the kid's DNA for testing."

Becker looked skyward. "It's probably *your* DNA, and it will 'mysteriously' match."

"How the hell would she get my DNA?"

"With you? It's probably on sale on the Internet."

Nate fried him with a look. "You're an idiot, you know that?"

"Sorry, but this time, I'm thinking you're the idiot, Ivory. Sic some lawyers on her and make her go away."

Nate shook his head. "If my family—especially my grandfather—got wind of a paternity issue? Shit. Nothing would give him more pleasure than to add to his troops, as he likes to refer to us."

Zeke shrugged. "So a kid might be just the ticket to showing Grandpa just how legit you can be, right?"

"I thought of that," Nate admitted. "But how shitty a move would that be, on every level?"

Becker's shoulders moved in a silent chuckle.

"What's so funny?" Nate demanded.

"You with a kid. If you don't think that's funny, then—"

"Shut the hell up."

Zeke held up a peacemaking hand. "Listen, you need a plan of attack," he said. "A strategy to get through this."

"And a lawyer," Becker added.

"You're right," he agreed, more with Zeke than Becker. "First up, I have to find out more about this Carrie chick. I did try to find her after that night but only because she…" He shook his head, hating the admission. "Had a video camera."

Becker moaned, dropping his head into his hand in disgust. "A *sex tape*, Ivory? That'll really help us get more investors for this project."

"It's five years old and quite possibly—hopefully—destroyed by now. But at the time, I wanted to get it back, but I couldn't find her or anyone who knew her. Now I have more information."

"So cruise down to Key West and have a look around," Becker said. "And take your new friend with you. Keep your enemies close, I always say."

Nate nodded. The suggestion—even though it was Becker's—made a lot of sense.

"And put her on the spot, test her a little," Zeke suggested. "Find out what she's made of and if she'd pull a stunt like this. She says she doesn't want money, so what does she want?"

"I'll tell you what you should do," Becker said, leaning forward as if an idea had grabbed hold of him. "Offer her a job."

"What?" the other two men asked in unison.

"No, I'm serious. That woman is plugged into the whole county system, and she can find her way around permits and waivers like no one else—she proved that with Frankie's land."

Frankie *had* introduced Liza as "the great unraveler of red tape." "We do need someone on staff who can handle that," he agreed, considering the idea. "But why would she want a job with me? She wants me to sign some form and disappear."

"Just offer the job," Becker said. "Make her an offer no normal County Clerk worker could refuse. Then you'll see if she's really serious about 'making a good life' for this kid."

"Damn, Becker, you took smart pills," Nate joked.

The other man gave a typically smart-ass Elliott Becker grin. "It's Frankie. She brings out a whole new me."

"Mandy does the same thing with me," Zeke admitted.

Nate looked skyward. "You guys are making me sick."

They just laughed, but then Zeke grew serious. "What about the DNA test?" he asked. "You going to do it?"

"I don't know." Truth was…the truth scared him. Absolute confirmation that he had a kid? "I have to figure it all out."

"Not at the expense of our stadium and team, I hope," Becker said. "Make sure your focus is where it should be: on the Barefoot Bay Bucks. We have a lot riding on this project, and we really need to rally some more investors."

"I know. I'll figure it all out."

"You will," Zeke said as they all stood to end breakfast. "Don't forget to—"

Something bright green whizzed by and slammed into Zeke's chest, shutting them all up as a Frisbee clattered to the table. They reacted with surprised laughs and turned at the sound of loud, fast footsteps. Two sets, in fact, both quite small. Two children approached, a tiny blond girl with her hand over her mouth and a matching tow-headed boy.

"Sorry," he said. "My sister…" He shook his head. "She didn't mean it. We're going to the beach, and she got excited."

He had to have been just about the same age as Dylan, Nate thought. "No problem, kiddo." Nate picked up the Frisbee and easily lobbed it to the boy, getting a grin when he clapped his hands over it and caught it.

"Emma! Edward!" A tall man in a white chef's coat came marching into the sunshine, a scowl on his face. "Don't bother the customers, you two. So sorry, gentlemen."

"No worries," Nate said. "We were just headed out."

He took a step closer, sizing up the two of them. "Twins?" he asked.

"I'm older by a minute," Edward said, making them all laugh.

The chef extended his hand to Nate. "I'm Chef Ian Browning, by the way. I know Mr. Nicholas and Mr. Becker, but don't believe we've met."

"Nathaniel Ivory." He wasn't used to introducing himself, since most people recognized him, but this man was obviously British and probably didn't read the tabloids much. "Cute kids," he added.

"Thanks." He reached the kids and put protective and proud hands on their shoulders. For a flash of an instant, Nate imagined what that would feel like. "The children's program doesn't start until nine, and my wife had to go over to the mainland," the chef said. "So, you're with the new baseball business, too? Everyone in my kitchen is talking about—Edward!"

The boy went zooming out of his father's grasp, followed by his sister.

"We're going to the beach!" she called out, her shyness gone as the two tore down the stairs to the sand.

"Wait!" The chef darted after them, throwing the men an exasperated smile as he chased his kids.

"Got your hands full, huh?" Nate asked as the man zipped by.

"And another on the way, mate." He disappeared onto the sand, leaving the three of them sharing a look.

"You ready for that?" Zeke asked wryly.

"Hell no."

"So be careful what you wish for...*mate*." Becker added the chef's English accent and grinned at Nate. "You just might find it."

Chapter Four

"Car, Aunt Liza? Now? N-O-W C-A-R!"

Liza tucked the dishtowel on the oven handle and smiled down at Dylan, her heart doing a little flip when she looked into his eyes—the very shade of tawny oak that had been haunting her every thought since the day before. Nate and Dylan did look so much alike. That fact was even more undeniable now that she'd seen Nate Ivory in person. Twenty-five years apart in age, but something in the eyes, the jaw, even the expression...had to be hereditary and not coincidence.

"Please?" Dylan dragged the word out, then frowned, no doubt wondering whether he could spell that one. "Now?"

"Yes. N-O-W." She nudged him to the kitchen door with one hand on his back, pausing at the dining room to call out, "Mom, I'm going to be in the driveway with Dylan!"

The announcement was a courtesy, but it didn't take away the fact that Liza still reported to her mom—thanks to the circumstances of her life—and she didn't like it.

After they unplugged the charger and maneuvered the bright red Power Wheels car into the driveway, Liza situated herself on the lawn where she could have an unobstructed view of the driveway, the street, and Dylan in his new toy.

"Do not go close to the street, Dylan," she warned as he climbed behind the wheel, his face bright in anticipation.

Mom had gotten him the Lightning McQueen electric car this past Christmas, and he lived for the chance to drive it, back and forth, in the semicircle driveway. That chance was usually the weekends, when Liza wasn't working. Mom watched him a few days, when she didn't have club meetings, lunches, tennis, or golf. Mostly, he was in day care, so Liza tried to spend every minute with him on the weekends.

"Here I go!" He gave it a little gas and started his circuit, waving each time he passed her.

She waved back, then leaned on her hands to look around the pristine neighborhood. Trimmed hibiscus, manicured emerald lawns, and rows of Queen palms lined the grid of streets that made up a painfully planned community full of pink and beige houses, all topped with the same barrel tile roof.

The sound of a car engine—a real one—made her open her eyes to check how close Dylan was to the street. Very.

"Careful," she called, though he was usually good about minding.

He stopped his little car suddenly, at the curb, and stood slowly. "C-A-R!"

"Yes, it's a car." She squinted into the sunshine, seeing a silver vehicle slowing as it approached her house. That was unusual in Blue Landing. Most of the retirees and snowbirds who populated the expensive development didn't even remember what it was like to have kids playing in the street. Living here was a great financial solution, and having her mother as a back-up for Dylan was convenient, but it sure wasn't the kid-friendly neighborhood she wanted.

Still, this driver was far more aware than most, slowing at her driveway.

"Wow!" Dylan slowly climbed out of his car, staring at the vehicle like it was a UFO. It was…different.

No, it was the sleek, space-age car she'd ridden in yesterday to the harbor. There couldn't be two cars that looked as if they'd been dipped in platinum and cost a million bucks.

Damn it all. *He'd found her.* Worse, he'd found Dylan, who walked toward the car parked in front of her mailbox.

Nate emerged like a god stepping out of his chariot, his hair streaked bronze in the sunlight, a loose white linen shirt accentuating his size and breadth.

Liza stood as dumbstruck as Dylan, her heart lodged firmly in her throat, denying her any chance to talk or breathe or demand to know what the hell he was doing here. But why bother asking that? She knew.

In two steps, she was behind Dylan, reaching a protective hand for his shoulder, but he shot away, running to the car.

"Car! Car! C-A-R."

A slow smile spread across Nate's face as he slipped off his sunglasses to get a better look. "You like it?" he asked Dylan.

"So pretty!"

Nate laughed, a low rumble of amusement that reached Liza's ears like a screaming alarm. He was already in love with Dylan, who, oblivious to any drama about to unfold, ran to the car and slapped his two hands on the curved spoiler in the back with a loud thwack. "Wow!"

Finally, Nate looked over to Liza, who had managed to swallow, find a shred of composure, and get to the end of the driveway.

"Hey," he said, the single word so simple and sexy and intrusive and intimate, she almost reeled.

Hey. *Hey*? Like it was no big deal that he'd hunted her down and come to her home and invaded her world *uninvited*?

"What are you doing here?"

"Aunt Liza!" Dylan answered for him. "Look!"

"I am looking," she said, her gaze flat on the car's owner and not the object of Dylan's fascination. "How did you find me?"

"Your address was on the paperwork you left." He turned his attention to Dylan, while Liza mentally kicked herself for the oversight. "You like cars, son?" he asked.

Son? Already? She must have choked a little, because Dylan turned to look at her, his eyes bright and his smile loopy.

"I love cars," he said.

So not fair. She'd told him that already. So, of course, he shows up in his one-of-a-kind classic something that someone with a Y chromosome could smell as special from a mile away.

"Well, maybe you can drive this one," Nate said to him.

This time, she choked loud and hard and

46

purposefully. "Excuse me," she said, lifting her chin and refusing to be the least bit distracted or deterred by his size and looks and overall hunkiness. "He's four and he can't drive."

"I see that." He angled his head. "But he likes cars."

Didn't he see that kind of ridiculous logic was why she was trying to keep Dylan from him? What else would he let a child do? "If you suggest my little boy drive a...whatever that is—"

"Aston Martin. I usually have one shipped to me when I'm staying somewhere more than a few weeks."

She closed her eyes, just letting that simple statement sum up everything about Nate Ivory. He had an Aston Martin shipped to him when he stayed somewhere.

"How is that even normal?"

He laughed at the question and jutted his chin to Dylan, who was prancing around the car, leaving smear prints on every window as he tried to see in. "He thinks it's normal. Will you, uh, introduce us?"

She considered refusing the request. She could. She was Dylan's legal guardian and, as such, she could determine who even talked to him, but... No, she wasn't that scared of Nate Ivory. And not that cruel. Plus, Dylan would have a full-out meltdown if that car suddenly disappeared.

"Dylan, honey, come here."

He slowly lifted his little face from the driver's window, where he'd been pressing so hard he probably had licked the glass by now.

"Come and meet Mr. Ivory."

Nate shot her a look. "You can call me Nate," he corrected as Dylan came forward. Nate crouched down to his size. "If you give me knuckles."

He held out his fist, and Dylan knew exactly what to do. The fist-bump came with that sweet smile and childish giggle. "Who are you?"

And that pure and honest curiosity.

"I'm..." He struggled with the word, and every cell in Liza's body seized up in fear of what he'd say next. She couldn't talk or jump in or even move as time stood still and she waited for...*your father*. "I'm a friend of your Aunt Liza's."

She let out an audible breath, and he stood slowly, his expression saying what his mouth wasn't. *Don't worry.*

But she was worried. How could she not? "So you just, what, decided to cruise into Blue Landing for fun today?"

He looked around. "I could tell you're conservative, Liza, but I wouldn't have put you quite in the middle of Disney World."

"We're living with my mother right now," she said. "We've been staying here for a year." Did she have to explain her personal situation to him? Well, he was Dylan's father. "My mom lived alone in this big house and so, well, you know what they say."

"There's no place like home with your mother?" he suggested with a teasing smile.

"It takes a village to raise a kid."

He glanced around. "Pretty sedate village."

Irritation skittered as a need to defend the little development rose, but he was right. "It's also safe, secure, and comes with a backup babysitter who loves Dylan almost as much as I do."

"Car! Car! C-A-R!" Dylan had returned to his inspection, bored by the adults talking.

"I told you he's kind of obsessed with spelling." Liza

tried to shift her attention to the little boy, but it was hard to stop looking at Nate. He looked different today, somehow. Calmer and more in control—but then, he'd ambushed her this time instead of the other way around.

"That's cute," he said, stepping closer to the car.

"Dwive!" Dylan insisted.

So Dylan had heard Nate suggest that. "Why would you plant that idea in his head?" she asked.

"Because it's what I'd want to do."

Dylan kept banging on the window and jumping up and down, until Nate opened the door. Little legs and arms scrambled right in, just as Mom came out of the front door.

"Liza?"

"Brace yourself," she whispered to Nate. "My mother is going to gush over you."

"Does she know about…Carrie and me?"

The question threw her a little. She hadn't expected him to care about things like that, or worry about how this affected her life in any way. A little knot of appreciation tightened in her chest.

"Nothing. You're going to be a total surprise. And I have to warn you, my mother has two weaknesses—she can't keep a secret, and she's a serial social climber. She'll tell everyone at the country club, on Facebook, and possibly stop by the local news stations to tell them that you were here. So, if she knows *why*…" She shook her head. "I'm not responsible for the ensuing scandal."

He put a light hand on her shoulder. "I got this." Instantly, a smile broke across his face as he turned to her mother. "Mrs. Lemanski?"

He's *got* this? He got her name wrong, for one thing. She hadn't been Mrs. Lemanski for…three husbands.

But the wrong name didn't make Mom stumble on her Manolos. The face she was staring at did. "Are you..." She put her hand on her chest, red nails gleaming. "Oh my God, are you..."

"Nathaniel Ivory."

Color rose from her heavy gold chain necklace right up to her perfectly styled frosted hair, her eyes popping. "As I live and breathe." She tapped her chest as though she couldn't do either one at the moment. "What on earth...oh, you are even better looking in real life! Gorgeous! Isn't he, Liza?"

"Stunning," she agreed dryly, getting a quick look from Nate.

"It's a pleasure to meet you." He held out his hand, and Mom practically lunged at it with both of hers, pumping mightily.

"Don't tell me you're moving into Blue Landing!"

Liza snorted. That'd be the day. He probably had servants' quarters nicer than this.

"I'm just here to see your daughter," he said. "I guess she didn't tell you we met at the press conference in Barefoot Bay yesterday."

"Oh, I read about that baseball team and..." Her mother finally took her eyes off Nate long enough to finally focus on Liza. "I thought you were at work. What were you doing there?"

Tracking down Dylan's biological father. "Uh, I—"

"Job hunting," Nate supplied. "And I'm here to deliver the good news. You're hired."

She just stared at him, utterly speechless.

"For what?" her mother asked.

"Yeah, for what?" Liza repeated.

He looked at her like she knew exactly what for. "My

50

administrative assistant. We were so impressed with how you helped Frankie Cardinale navigate all that county red tape, we decided unanimously to offer you a job."

She tried—she really did—to say something, but not a word would come out. *I got this* meant offering her a job? "Are you out of your mind?" she asked under her breath.

But her mother heard. "Are *you*?" she demanded of Liza. "This is the best news in…well, forever! You say every day how miserable you are at the County Clerk's office and, Liza…" Her eyes darted to Nate, stealing a glance at his body and lingering over…all of it. "I mean, *Liza*. Why would you not accept?"

"Because…" It was insanity. Working for him? Was this his way of staying around Dylan? "I don't know the pay or benefits or—"

"Name your price," Nate said. "We'll triple your current salary, cover health care and—"

Dylan honked the horn lightly, making Nate smile.

"And there's a children's program at the resort where I'm setting up the office until we get further along on the site. Dylan can be in it at our expense."

"Liza!" Her mom practically squealed. "It's an answer to your prayers!"

"I wasn't praying for another job." Except that she kind of was. What she wasn't praying for was any reason to be near Nate Ivory. In fact, the opposite was far, far preferable.

"What do you say?" he asked.

Before she answered, Dylan laid on the horn with all he had, the deafening blare echoing over the quiet neighborhood.

Liza leaped at the excuse, rushing to the driver's door

to stop the noise. "Dylan!" In the seat, his eyes were wild as he pressed the steering wheel with all his might.

"Stop!" she cried, lifting his hand for blessed silence. "Sorry, Nate." She tried to extricate Dylan from the seat, but his little hands clamped on the steering wheel, and he started kicking wildly, his sneakers slamming into the bottom of the dashboard, leaving tiny black scuffs on the cream-colored leather. "Dylan, stop that!"

"I want to dwive!" Smack, smack, scuff, scuff.

"Dylan, please."

"*Dwiiiiiive!*" He wailed, his voice rising exponentially from upset to temper tantrum. Full-blown meltdown was about fifteen seconds away. Actually, it might have already arrived.

She bit her lip, not sure whether to laugh or reprimand. *Welcome to fatherhood, Nate Ivory. How would this sound in Beverly Hills?*

Nate was next to her before she realized what was happening, large, strong hands reaching into the car to easily calm the kicking. "Take it easy, bud."

Dylan kicked harder.

"You can drive it."

And then he stopped. Liza whipped around to look at him, her breath taken away by how close he was, their shoulders touching. "Don't encourage him. He'll just be more disappointed. He's only four, Nate."

"I know, and such a big guy." He gave Dylan's legs a squeeze. "When's your birthday, bud?"

"Januawy twenty-fuhst!" He started kicking again, like it was his birthday all over again.

Nate seemed to pale for a split second—no doubt, the car had never been treated like this—but then he took

52

control of the wild legs again, a catch in his voice. "Not if you kick."

Dylan stopped instantly. Because kids were traitors like that.

"And only if Aunt Liza says yes," Nate added.

"Aunt Liza, pleeeeease!"

"I don't…no. You can't take him in this car."

"I want to dwive!" Dylan screamed again.

Nate covered the boy's legs again. "In a minute—"

"No." Liza reached in and firmly took hold of Dylan, shouldering Nate out of the way. "Just no." He wasn't going to blow in here and do this. "You can't give a child everything he wants, and you can't make promises you can't keep." With a tight grip, she got Dylan out of the seat. "You can't let him drive." Her voice rose as she wrestled with a writhing, squirming, unhappy forty-two pounds of wild child. "And you can't..." *Take him away from me.* Which was really at the bottom of the low-grade panic rising in her chest.

Dylan kicked her thigh so hard she almost buckled.

"Liza." The reprimand and surprise in her mother's voice were loud and clear. Instantly, she was there, trying to wrest Dylan from her arms. "What's gotten into you?"

"Me? What about—"

"I want to *dwiiiiiive!*"

Sweat prickled under her arms, and all Liza's muscles bunched as she tried to still Dylan, looking over his shoulder to meet Nate's amused gaze. "You think this is funny?" she asked him.

"I think you're overreacting. Put him down, and let's all take a ride."

"There are two seats, Nate."

"Go, go." Her mother practically pushed her from behind. "I'll stay here, and you three go for a little zip around the neighborhood. You can talk about your new job. What are the hours?" she asked.

Oh, *Lord.*

"She can set her own." He slipped behind the wheel, touching something that made the seat shift way back, at least ten inches from the steering wheel. He reached out for Dylan. "Let's take a drive, tiger."

Dylan practically flew out of Liza's arms. "I dwive! I dwive!"

"Yep, you can drive." With an easy movement, Nate took Dylan from her arms and slid him behind the wheel. "You coming, Liza?"

"Aunt Liza!" Dylan cried, kicking again as excitement overtook his whole body. "Let's go!"

"You heard the boy, let's go." Nate had the nerve to grin at her as he pulled the seat belt across Dylan's little body, nestling the child into place on his lap.

On a sigh, she started around the back of the car, her mom instantly on her heels. "Liza! This is a miracle, isn't it?"

Not exactly.

"This job sounds wonderful." She squeezed Liza's hands. "And do you know he's one of the most eligible billionaires in the country? Billionaires *with a b,* Liza."

"Don't get your hopes up, Mom. This isn't about...us."

"Health benefits! Child care! Set your own hours!" Mom's voice rose with every empty promise. Because, really, what else could they be? "And look at him! You wouldn't be the first boss-and-secretary romance."

She looked to the sky, a full-headed eye roll necessary to calm her mother on a marriage roll.

"Let's go," Nate called. "I can't hold him still much longer."

"And he's so good with kids!" Mom slapped her hands on her cheeks in sheer wonder.

How good would he seem in a custody battle?

The words had a chilling effect on her heart, making her step toward the car to protect what was hers. Dylan was hers.

She couldn't forget that.

Except…he was also Nate's.

Chapter Five

As soon as the car was moving, Dylan relaxed into Nate, his tiny hands gripping the leather steering wheel, his little body finally still.

His guardian, on the other hand, was anything but relaxed. He threw her a reassuring look, but she had that lip trapped between her teeth again, her arms wrapped around herself as tight as the seat belt.

"There we go, now, we're going to make a right." Of course, Nate controlled the car completely, still holding the wheel with his own two hands and keeping them at a nice ten miles an hour on completely empty streets. "You got it, kid."

He felt Liza's stern look and met it with another smile. "S'okay, Aunt Liza," he said softly. "We got this."

"Like you had it back there at my house?" she asked under her breath. "With some bogus job offer?"

"We got this!" Dylan repeated in his high-pitched voice. A voice that reached into Nate's heart and twisted things around a little.

"Not bogus at all," he replied. "The offer is legit."

"Why?" she asked.

"Because you're exactly what we need and…" Dylan squirmed and giggled and stole a glance of pure joy over his shoulder. Because maybe he wanted to be near this kid? "It makes sense."

No, it didn't actually make sense, but he couldn't deny the sensation that had rocked him at the sight of Dylan Cassidy.

God uses the same flawless mold for every piece of Ivory glass!

He could hear the Colonel's proud voice, his announcement made at each birth and baptism in the Ivory family, celebrating the growth of the name built on the glass industry.

"It's just crazy," Liza said.

Yes, it was. But…it was true. And Dylan looked like he'd walked right out of that mold.

"Whoa, here comes a truck." Nate inched the wheel to the right and hugged the curb while a pickup rolled by.

"T-R-U-C-K! Truck."

"And what a great speller!" Nate gave the boy's shiny hair a ruffle, remembering his own hair being that honey color when he was small.

"Many words," Liza agreed. "But he shouldn't win when he has a temper tantrum."

"Does he have them often?"

She blew out a breath. "All the time. Daily. Hourly. Way more than you want to deal with, trust me."

He wanted to laugh, but he got her message. She didn't want him to like this child.

"He'll kick the heck out of your car," she added. "And he never sleeps through the night. Plus, he gets a lot of colds and…" Her gaze shifted to Dylan's face, and her eyes deepened in color, more blue with concern. "And he's..." She nibbled her lip. "He's a good kid," she finished.

"I'm sure, but—let's wait here for the mailman to pass, bud."

"M-A-I-L! Mail!" Dylan shimmied on Nate's lap, so delighted with himself. "Aunt Liza, I can dwive!"

The childish pronunciation and babyish enthusiasm were so damn sweet, Nate couldn't help but smile. But Liza's misery was apparent with every passing minute. "Just one more street, then we go back to your..." He had no idea what this child called Liza's mother.

"Just Paulette," she supplied. "And be prepared for half of the Gulf Shore Country Club to be waiting on the front lawn with cameras when we get back."

And how long until one of those amateur paparazzi calls the professionals in and someone takes a look at the kid and Nate only to put two and two together and come up with a new Ivory scandal?

One look at Liza, and he knew she was thinking the same thing. "I should probably lie low," he said.

"Ya think?"

"S-T-O-P! Stop!"

"Yep," Nate agreed, tapping the brakes at the intersection and waiting for a second before they continued on. He should probably stop, too. Stop soaking up this child and already imagining...a relationship.

He put a hand on the tiny shoulder in front of him, a dark, hollow sensation in his gut, a lone question burning since this news first broke. Was it possible he really had a son?

He pulled back into the driveway and turned off the

car, relieved not to see a bevy of local socialites waiting for him. "Here you go, Dylan," he said, unlatching the seat belt and opening the door.

"Pauwette!" Dylan hollered, then ran toward the house, leaving them alone in the car.

After watching the boy disappear and leave behind a singularly confusing hole in Nate's heart, he had to pose the question that had been haunting him.

"Why wouldn't she find me and tell me?" he asked softly, knowing his voice was rich with pain and really not caring. The realization hurt.

"She did."

"She did not," he fired back. "I swear on anything and everything that journal she wrote is a lie. I never saw her again, and she…" A low anger seethed and bubbled in his veins. "What kind of person decides she has a right to keep that secret?"

He expected a defense of her dearly departed friend, but Liza lifted her shoulders and shook her head. "A person who wants to keep her child. She was afraid you and your family would want him."

"That's what she said in the notebook, which is riddled with lies."

"No, she told me that from the beginning," Liza said. "I always thought the father should have signed something, but she wouldn't do that. She was convinced you'd take the baby or your family would."

And she'd be right. Mimsy and the Colonel would pay whoever needed to be paid and sign whatever needed to be signed and weather whatever shitstorm the media threw at them, because Ivorys stuck together, no matter what.

"And would that have been a legitimate fear?" Liza asked when he didn't answer.

Nate looked at her for a long time, debating exactly what to say. In the end, he chose a simple course of action—his other reason for coming here today.

"I want to find out more about her," he said.

"I can tell you what you need to know."

He shook his head. "I don't think that girl I met and the one you knew were the same."

"What?"

"I mean, they might be the same person, but she was obviously a chameleon or split personality or something."

"Maybe she was," she admitted. "But that doesn't change this mess of a situation."

"Liza, I didn't go looking for this."

She closed her eyes and nodded. "I shouldn't have—"

"Oh, yes, you should have," he corrected. "A man has a right to know if he's had a child, and your friend was the one who made a huge mistake, not you."

"I agree," she said. "Except, she always said she'd told the father of her baby that she was pregnant and he told her to get lost."

"That conversation never happened with me," he said, a little tired of making this assertion. "Maybe Dylan's not mine."

"But her journal! She uses your name, describes your meeting exactly as you said it happened."

"Liza, she wouldn't be the first woman to fantasize about..." He realized how arrogant the statement sounded, and let his voice trail off. "I have some, I don't know what you'd call them, admirers? Fans?

Desperate women who like my last name and want it."

She snorted softly. "Trust me, Carrie wasn't that woman."

"Like I said, I need to find out just who and what she was," he said.

"I know who she was, Nate. She lived with me for three and a half years. We were close friends, we talked about everything, we raised her child together, we...what?" She'd finally seen his look.

"She didn't tell you my name, though, right? She left it in some notebook that you found when she died? Did you ever meet her family?"

"Her parents were dead, and she was an only child."

"You really know nothing about her except what she fabricated since she moved here."

She closed her eyes, unable to deny that. "She never seemed anything but one hundred percent genuine."

"Are you a good judge of character?"

She didn't answer at first, then lifted a shoulder in admission. "I'm a better judge of things on paper, I'll admit. I can spot a phony legal document a mile away, but..." She sighed. "I do things impulsively, and maybe I trust too easily."

He put his hand over hers, a sympathy he didn't quite understand but couldn't deny taking hold. "Let's do a little investigating, then. Maybe my friend who lives in Key West can help, too. We both deserve to know the truth."

"Remember, I work in the County Clerk's office, and that gives me access to a lot of official documents, from every county in the country. I can dig into that name, Bailey Banks, and of course, more about her parents and childhood in Arizona."

"If she was even from there. Sorry, Liza, but everything about her is suspect. Is she even really dead?"

Liza closed her eyes. "I identified her body after the accident."

"I'm sorry." He added some pressure to her hand, wanting her to know he meant that. "How did Dylan handle that?"

"Not well," she said. "He misses her, although I think he's forgetting about her as each month passes. He's always had me, and my mother, who adores him. I've been like a mother to him from the day he was born." She slipped her hand out from underneath Nate's, taking a second to nibble on her lip as she chose her next words carefully. "I need you to know something."

He nodded, waiting.

"I won't give him up easily, no matter what we find out about Carrie or what a DNA test says or what you want to do. I will fight for him because I love him with every cell in my body. His mother named me legal guardian, and that will carry a lot of weight in court."

Court? "The last thing I want to do is drag this to court."

"Then sign the paper and let me have him to raise and love," she said. "You can..." She closed her eyes as if the words pained her. "You can see him."

Two responses played in his head. *Maybe I will* was one. The other was the truth, so he said it. "He's an Ivory."

"What does that mean?" she demanded.

"It means he's...family."

"Define family," she shot back. "I've been with him since he took his first breath, first step, first bath and first birthday. I rock him to sleep every night. I take him to the park and supervise playdates and make sure he eats right. Except for a few strands of DNA, I *am* his mother."

"And because of a few strands of DNA, I could be his father."

For a long time, they just stared at each other, neither one willing or able to say a word. He studied her mysterious eyes, dark with distrust and fear and more alluring and beautiful than anything he could remember seeing in a long time.

"Why are you smiling?" she asked.

Was he? "I don't know. I guess because you're so pretty."

She inched back. "Now? You're going to hit on me now in the middle of the biggest crisis of either one of our lives?"

"I'm not hitting on you, Liza. Though I do wish we'd met under different circumstances."

"Like what? A party on your yacht? What did you say? Bare-ass naked with some guy's wife's hand on your—"

"Shhh." He put his finger over her lip to stop the words from spewing out. For reasons he'd never, ever understand, a low burn of embarrassment started in his gut. He didn't want this lovely, caring, maternal young woman, who clearly gave with all her heart and soul, to even think about his…*lifestyle*.

"Listen, Key West is a couple of hours away on my boat. Let's go together and see what we can find out about her."

For a second, he was sure she was about to say no to the invitation, but then she stunned him with a direct look and a simple answer. "Yes, I'll go."

After they exchanged numbers and made plans for him to pick her up the next day, she climbed out of the car, pointedly not issuing an invitation for him to come inside. Instead, she walked slowly away from his car.

Then her front door flew open, and Nate glanced back to see Dylan running toward the street, arms outstretched. "N-A-T-E! I spell your name! N-A-T-E!"

The letters were screamed so loud, he heard them through the closed windows. Liza scooped the child up in her arms to carry him in without even looking back at Nate's car.

She was his mother, for all intents and purposes. But if he was his father…he simply had to know. And then?

He had no idea.

Chapter Six

He sent a limo for her. And a remote-control-operated toy sports car for Dylan. Liza didn't know whether to be thrilled or disappointed, but she was a little of both when the driver closed the door with a solid thud. With Mom waving goodbye from the driveway and Dylan dancing with excitement for his new toy, Liza dropped her head back on the cool leather and closed her eyes.

Everything smelled…rich. Was this just like the limo where he and Carrie…

Don't, Liza. Don't think about that.

This would be a fact-finding mission, a day trip to the Keys and back, a chance to smooth out the wrinkles in this messy situation. This trip was so impersonal that he sent a car and driver rather than picking her up himself. She had to remember that and put her mother's musings and any of her own really stupid secret fantasies to sleep while she focused on finding out what they could about Carrie Cassidy.

She held on to that thought until the limo driver pulled into the harbor on Mimosa Key and the first thing she saw was Nathaniel Ivory waiting on the dock next to the cabin cruiser she'd been on yesterday.

Bathed in sunshine, the breeze whipping his hair into a tousled mess, he stood with his hands on narrow hips, wearing khakis and a faded blue button-down shirt that fit his broad shoulders like it was custom-made for him—well, duh. Everything was custom-made for him.

His sleeves were rolled up to show corded forearms, the top button undone to reveal a peek of that impressive chest. His thick hair brushed the collar of his shirt with a hint of wave, the sun picking up the strands of burnished gold among the much darker shades.

He looked unreal, like a Photoshopped model who'd just stepped off the pages of a Nautica ad.

Who wouldn't buy what he was selling?

He approached the limo and opened the door before the driver even got out, dipping over to give her a dazzling smile. "Hope you don't mind the ride."

She laughed. "Yeah, all this leather and luxury. Really sucks."

"I wanted to get you, but I had some things I had to take care of on board." He reached for her hand to help her out, glancing up to the driver as he got out of the front. "Is her bag in the back?"

"My bag?" Liza stepped into the sunshine, warmed by it and the thought that he expected her to bring a bag. "Won't we be back tonight?"

"It's about a four-hour cruise down there, and I don't know how long it will take us to poke around Key West, and there might be some weather tonight."

Was he proposing they get a hotel or sleep on his boat? It was sizable, but she'd seen only one cabin. She leaned around his shoulder to check out the vessel again. "It looks pretty seaworthy to me."

"Good Lord, Liza, I wouldn't take you to the Keys on that." With a strong hand on her shoulder, he turned her to look beyond the harbor to the open water. "We're taking my *other* boat."

She couldn't do anything but stare. "I thought that was…" A freaking cruise ship. "Someone else's."

"*N'Vidrio*? I've been practically living on her for years."

It was a floating castle of a super-mega-over-the-top yacht, complete with colorful flags and a helicopter pad. "What does the name mean? Other than 'biggest boat in the damn ocean'?"

He laughed. "It's not. N for Nate. *Vidrio* is Spanish for glass, which is the basis of my family's fortune, and it's also close to the word for envy."

"Which everyone feels when they see that yacht." She turned back to the thirty-foot cabin cruiser. "And this is what? Your ferry boat?"

"Precisely. There's a utility garage on the lower deck of the yacht to house this."

His *utility boat* was nicer than some vessels the millionaires in Naples had. "Well, I didn't bring a bag," she finally said, still trying to get her head around the fact that she was going to the Keys on *that yacht*.

"No worries. We have everything you need on board. My sister, Beth, travels with me a lot, so her stateroom is full of anything a woman needs, and you're about the same size. If not, we can have some clothes delivered. There are personal shoppers in Key West."

Of course there were. She gave a smile and let it slide into a soft laugh. "Your life," she said, shaking her head, "is not like anything I've ever imagined."

"Then relax and enjoy it," he said, guiding her toward

the boat. "Let's try to think of this as an adventure rather than a mission."

By the time they pulled out of the harbor, Liza started to relax. The breeze picked up, just chilly enough to make her glad she wore a sweater, and the briny smells of the sea made her enjoy a deep inhale and the rumble of high-octane inboard motors behind her.

An adventure rather than a mission.

Could she get that mind-set for this excursion? She peeked out from under her lashes to watch Nate steer them toward his yacht, enjoying the view of him as much as the glorious day on the water. It certainly was…adventurous.

How did a person actually *live* like this?

Every minute made her more convinced that she couldn't let Dylan be sucked into this life. There was nothing normal about it. Everything about Nate was too big, too much, too rich, too wild.

Nate angled the wheel and brought the boat around to aim right at the massive white vessel. Four stories and well over a hundred feet long, gleaming white with glossy black windows, *N'Vidrio* was nothing short of breathtaking.

"Wow."

He turned from the helm as they motored up to the back end of the yacht and two men in matching navy shirts came out to greet them. "It does have a wow factor," he conceded. "But most of the time, it's just home for me."

She stood and joined him, shouldering her handbag and bracing her legs for the docking. "Do you really live here?"

"When I am traveling near water, yeah. But the

harbor in Mimosa Key is too small, so I keep it out here. I'm opening an office in the resort, as you know, so I'll split my time between here and there."

Because living at a resort was more normal than on a megayacht. One of the crewmen helped her on board, and Nate joined her, giving her a guided tour through the first deck, then the second, and by the time they reached the main living level, she'd seen so much leather and brass and marble and crystal, her head was spinning.

He took her to the bridge and introduced her to Captain Vicary, whose warmth and experience immediately put Liza at ease. After that, they moved to a private outdoor lounge with a Jacuzzi, a dining table, and a bar—staffed, of course, by another navy-shirted crew member.

"I ordered some lunch," he said as they settled across from each other on white leather lounge chairs. "Would you like a drink?"

When in Rome, right? "I'll have what you're having."

He stepped away and spoke to the bartender, leaving Liza alone for a moment. She soaked up the view, caressed the butter-soft lounge chair, and then opened her bag to see if she had any texts from Mom.

She did, a picture of Dylan and his new car.

When Nate came back with two Bloody Marys, she turned the phone for him to see. "Thank you, by the way. He was in heaven."

"C-A-R?" he asked, smiling at the picture.

"Spelled so many times, I couldn't wait to get in the L-I-M-O."

He handed her the drink and sat across from her,

holding his for a toast. "Here's to Dylan, then. He's a great kid."

She didn't drink right away, gauging exactly what the wistfulness in his voice could mean. "You're still thinking about it, aren't you?"

He sipped, lifting a brow. "About him being mine and what that means? Of course. That's why we're here, right? To find out the truth about...her."

"You can't even say her name."

"I don't know what it was, evidently," he shot back. "She wasn't really my type."

She let out a soft grunt. "But that didn't stop you from—"

He held up his hand, palm out, silencing her. "I don't think my bad choices are a big surprise to anyone, including you. For what it's worth, I'm trying—and succeeding—to change my wicked ways."

"No more casual limo hookups?" she asked. "Why?"

He picked up the glass and studied the red liquid, toying with the leaves of the crisp celery stick garnish. "Those days are over." He slipped into a rueful smile. "They have to be."

She sat a little straighter, not sure what he was saying. Was it because of Dylan? "Why?"

"Because of..." He shook his head. "Look, Liza, I've had a good time. A professional partier. A wild lifestyle. But I've made a promise to settle down, and I plan on keeping it."

"A promise to who?"

"The Colonel." He shrugged, as if she might not know who that was. "Also known as 'Grandfather,' but he really hates to be called that. Thinks it sounds too soft."

She knew the famous patriarch of the Ivory clan, married to "Mimsy," as they called his eighty-year-old wife, both as famous as the king and queen of a country. "So you promised your grandparents, not your parents?" she asked.

"My parents?" He let out a dry laugh, then took a deep drink. "My mother lives in Belgium, a virtual recluse. My father is on his…fourth wife? I lost track and can't stand any of them. But suffice it to say he's in no position to pass judgment on how I live my personal life. No, the only opinion that matters in our family is that of one old ex-Marine who has some very impressive purse strings."

She couldn't help curling her lip. "That's kind of sad, don't you think?"

"What's sad is the Colonel thinking I'm a waste of the Ivory name." A wholly different kind of wistfulness colored his tone, surprising her.

"So you're cleaning up your act?" she asked. When he nodded, she added, "What's driving that? The purse strings or what your grandfather might think?"

"Not the purse strings. I have my trust fund, and no one can take it from me. No, it's his opinion that matters to me," he admitted.

Liza shifted on the lounge chair, taking a minute to have another spicy sip, letting the sunshine and alcohol and surprising confessions warm her. "For as much cyberstalking, as you call it, that I've done, I don't know much about your grandfather. He doesn't get as much media coverage as the rest of you."

"That's because he's the behind-the-scenes manipulator."

"Is that how he got so rich?"

He lifted his Bloody Mary and tapped the side. "This made him rich."

Ivory Glass was one of the most well-known brands in the world, as common as Kleenex and Coca-Cola. "Did he invent it?" she asked.

"Actually, his father did. The first James Ivory was a glassblower in Upstate New York at the turn of the twentieth century. He created the compound that made the glass nearly unbreakable but didn't do much with it. When my grandfather was still in the Marines, working his way up the ranks after the war, he already knew his dad was sitting on a pile of gold. By the time he left the military as a colonel, he didn't let the wound that gave him a lifelong limp stop him. The post-World War II building boom happened, he mined that gold, making sure Ivory glass windows went into every new skyscraper in America. The rest is family history."

A history she knew in rough detail. The Colonel and his wife had six overachiever kids and they had kids. Everyone in the family either stayed in the business as it sat on top of the *Fortune* 500 list or went on to politics, entertainment, finance, real estate, or business.

"Ivory always turns to gold," she said, quoting a common expression about the family.

"Or a party." He set the glass down with a thud. "But, like I said, I'm out to change that."

"Is that why you've taken this role as the manager of the Barefoot Bay Bucks?"

"One of the reasons. Starting a minor-league team, building a stadium, yeah, the project has really given me a focus, and I'm stoked for the job and working with such good friends. But there are more steps in my non-evil plan." He made a sweeping grand gesture toward the yacht. "You might notice the distinct lack of dancing girls and drinking boys, also known as the regulars on *N'Vidrio*."

"Dancing girls?"

"A euphemism for…"

"The blondes in the hot tub you referred to the other day."

He didn't answer right away, but his golden-brown gaze turned warm as he regarded her. "I don't even like blondes."

Heat curled through her, unexpected and unwanted and way, way too strong. She should look away. She should make a quip or stand up or remind him that Carrie was a blonde. She should do a lot of things other than stare right back for five, six, seven straight heartbeats.

Holy hell, she realized with a start. *I could like this man.*

In fact, she already did.

When they were close to Key West, the captain tracked south around Tank Island to work the ship to one of the few docks near town large enough to accommodate her. Nate was taking Liza to the bridge to enjoy the process of watching Vicary in action, when his chief steward signaled him for a private conversation.

"Excuse me, sir," Alex said in a soft voice. "Colonel Ivory is calling your stateroom."

A call from his grandfather was rare, but not entirely

unexpected. Sometimes, the old man had to "spend time in the trenches," as he liked to say. "Have him hold, Alex. I'll be right there."

"Do you have to go?" Liza asked when the steward walked away.

"For a few minutes. Go up to the bridge, and I'll meet you there. Captain Vicary will make you feel at home."

"I doubt I'd ever feel at home here," she said. "But take your time, and I'll enjoy the scenery."

He followed another corridor to the oversized master stateroom that took up nearly half of the second deck. Taking a deep breath, he sat in a plush office chair and picked up the satellite phone.

"Hello, Colonel."

"Key West, young man? That's never a good place for you. Bad as Vegas, in my opinion. Why don't you go somewhere less colorful?"

Nate smiled to himself, not at all surprised at the greeting. "I'm entertaining a young woman—"

"Of course you are."

"—who we are hiring to work as an admin for the baseball team."

He harrumphed. "Don't get your milk where you get your bread, son. It's bad form."

It was impossible not to laugh at him. "I'll take your counsel, sir. Is that why you're calling?"

"I'm calling because we haven't seen you in over a month. Mimsy gets anxious, you know, and wants as full a table as possible for our family meal. Sunday dinner is critical time for the family."

Critical for bonding or for the Colonel to stick his nose into the business of every one of them? Both, Nate knew. Every Ivory who could make it was expected to show up at the "Ivory Tower" in "full uniform"—suit and tie for the men, formal dress for the women. It was tedious as hell, but they all knew better than to ignore too many Sundays and risk a surprise visit from the Colonel. "Maybe in a few weeks, sir. I'm really tied up with this new venture."

"If I know you, you're tied up, all right. To the bedpost with this female friend."

"Actually, you're wrong. She's not…" Well, she *was* hot. And he had been thinking about kissing her for the entire trip, but…they had too many complications. "She's got a kid."

"Really? Nothing wrong with that, long as you make your own."

Evidently, he had. He didn't answer, his gaze moving to the open view of Key West out his sliding glass door.

"Listen to me, Nathaniel." Nate knew what the softening of his voice meant. The Colonel often used a different tone when he really wanted to make sure his point got across. "I'm watching for that progress you promised. You know I'm not getting any younger."

He was eighty-three, going on fifty. "I know, sir."

"And no matter what situation you get yourself into, you can depend on your family—especially me—to help you."

"Thank you, sir." He thought about Dylan for a moment, longing to tell the Colonel more about the boy and the situation. It would be so easy to bring Dylan into the Ivory clan. He'd be accepted and loved and, regardless of what Liza thought, he'd be brought up right.

Shit, what a mess. "I'll be in touch with you, sir," he added vaguely.

They finished the conversation after a moment, and Nate headed back to the bridge, but before he turned the corner, he heard the pretty, musical notes of Liza laughing.

The impact brought him to a halt, making him realize how rare a sound that was. And how much he wanted to hear more of it. She had laughed over lunch, but she'd been cautious, asking a lot of questions about his family, keeping the subject on him and not her. Now he realized, with a little regret, he'd found out very little about her. And everything in him wanted to change that.

He came around the corner, and she was still laughing with the captain, but her face flushed slightly. "Everything okay?" she asked, her laughter fading.

No, he thought with a start. This wasn't okay. Every minute with her, things just got more complicated. "Yeah, yeah, I'm fine. Just…work things. You want to walk to the bow and watch the docking? It's a lot of fun from up there."

"It's fun from here, too," Captain Vicary said with a flirtatious wink at Liza. "But you can take her."

Without thinking—well, maybe he thought a little— Nate reached for her hand. "Careful, he'll have you working here if you show any interest in yachting at all."

She settled her pretty gaze on the captain. "We were just talking about that."

"She's working for me," he said, pulling her hand into his chest. "And it's time we finalize that arrangement right now."

She let him guide her around to the bow, their feet tapping the teak deck in unison. "He's a lady killer, you know that," Nate said.

"Captain Vicary?" Once again, the infectious laugh.

"He let me steer for a while. It was great. I got us around that island all by myself."

He laughed. "With the help of a crew and a few engines, not to mention radar navigation. But I agree, it's a kick to drive this thing." And so was putting his hands on her waist and getting behind her, guiding her up the last narrow set of stairs to the tip of the bow.

There, he stayed right behind her, close enough that her body molded into his and the wind blew her hair against his cheeks.

"I swear I won't make a 'king of the world' joke," he teased.

She tilted her head back just enough to catch his gaze. "But you are king of the world, Nate Ivory. And this thing is damn near as big as the *Titanic*."

"But more seaworthy, I hope." The wind lifted more of her hair, and he reached out and got a handful, sliding it to the side to revel in the shape of her bare neck. And a sudden bloom of chills on her skin. "Are you cold, Liza?"

Her body, just close enough to his so that he could feel her from shoulders to thighs, relaxed a little. "Anything but."

"Good." He studied those chill bumps and the tiny dark hairs on the nape of her neck, fighting a very strong desire to lean forward a few inches and plant one little kiss on that smooth, smooth skin.

"You know what you are, Liza?" He dragged one finger over the skin, making her shudder.

"I bet I seem terribly pedestrian to you."

"Pedestrian? That is not at all the word I was thinking right now." *Delicious. Inviting. Feminine.* "Why would you say that?"

77

She glanced over her shoulder at him. "I'm not made for this, you know. This…life. I'm really kind of simple and ordinary, and my idea of an exciting Saturday afternoon is a trip to the Germ Factory with Dylan."

"The Germ Factory?" He laughed. "What the hell is that?"

"A play place with bins of plastic balls for jumping. That's what I do, Nate. And during the week I straighten out documentation messes for the county. I don't…drink cocktails on yacht decks with billionaires."

"Well, you do today." He looked at her for a long moment, then gently touched her chin, directing her face forward. "Now watch how fantastic your buddy Vicary is at docking. He's going to take this thirty-foot-wide monster and slide it right there, between those two piers."

He felt her sigh, doing as he suggested, and letting herself slip a little closer to him. She fit perfectly there, so he rested his hands on her shoulders, and neither of them spoke, letting the sounds of the crew dropping the dock cushions on either side of the yacht and the low rumble of the engines fill the silence. A few birds squawked in greeting, somehow intensifying the tangy, briny smell of the sea.

An unexpected lurch made Liza fall into him before she grabbed the railing for stability.

"And speaking of straightening out documentation messes for the county…"

"Yes?"

"Are you taking the job as chief unraveler of red tape for my organization?"

Slowly, she turned, trapped by his body and the railing, the look on her face saying she either didn't believe him or…maybe she liked the idea. He couldn't tell.

"You know you want to, Liza." As much as he wanted to kiss her right that moment, to seal the deal.

"I'm not going to lie, Nate. I'm intrigued and interested. But…"

"No buts, say yes."

"Not yet," she replied.

He added a little more pressure, pulling her forward as if he could just impress upon her how fantastic this idea was. "Look, I'm lost in this job. I've never had a freaking job in my life. I don't want to fail, and you're…you're like a secret weapon. You've worked your whole life."

"You say that like it's some kind of true accomplishment instead of a jail sentence. Plus, Nate, I hate to break it to you, but out here in the real world, *everyone* works their whole life. That doesn't make me some kind of Wonder Woman."

"You are a Wonder Woman when it comes to land documents and official records. I'm going to work right at the Casa Blanca Resort until we get offices built on-site at the stadium, and it's beautiful there…"

He didn't have her, he could tell. She was definitely waffling between "you're out of your mind" and "no."

"And," he added with a smile he hoped charmed her, "they have that amazing kids program."

"I don't know."

"What don't you know?" he prodded. "It's perfect."

"I can't do anything until I know what's going to happen with Dylan. And how could you work with him around and…" She shook her head. "No. No. My goal with meeting you was to get rid of you, not get closer. I can't."

Without thinking, he pulled her into him, the very opposite of what she said she wanted.

She put her hands on his chest and looked up at him, those incredible sapphire and emerald eyes wide and serious. "You want to know something about me, Nate?"

"I actually want to know everything about you," he confessed.

She gave a vague smile. "Let's start with this, the thing I dislike the most about my…situation in life. The almost-not-quiteness of it."

"Excuse me?"

"It somehow always seems to haunt me. I almost-but-not-quite have an amazing son, but he's not, you know, mine. And I can't be sure he ever will be. I almost-but-not-quite have a beautiful, safe home in a nice development, except my mother owns it, and that makes her think she owns me. I almost-but-not-quite was in love once, too, but he…" She gave a dismissive wave. "Didn't work out. And now I almost-but-not-quite have the perfect job offer land in my lap, except it's…"

"It's what? It's not almost-quite anything. This is a bona fide offer."

"I can't spend that much time around you…with Dylan and…no."

Without thinking, he pulled her a little closer, just to erase the raw misery in those beautiful eyes.

"I *am* common and simple and pedestrian," she said softly, not lifting her arms to return the embrace but not pushing him away, either. "And I have very strong feelings about that child. I love him beyond description."

Her lower lip quivered just enough to show she was a little afraid of what he might say next. Or do. Because he couldn't stop looking at those lips and thinking about…

The ship lurched again, bumping the pier and slamming them together, his lips hitting right on hers in a completely unexpected kiss. For one flash of a second, neither moved, then they both slowly backed away.

He refused to apologize, and she just let a hint of a smile lift her lips. "You know what you just did, don't you?"

"Changed the dynamic between us?"

"You almost-but-not-quite kissed me." The smile grew. "The story of my life."

The boat stopped with a loud horn announcing their arrival and covering up his next sentence. "Might have to change that story, Liza."

Chapter Seven

The minute they stepped off the yacht to the pier, Nate pulled on a nondescript baseball cap. "Sorry," he muttered as he added his reflective shades. "Gotta suit up."

"I keep forgetting I'm with a celebrity."

He snorted derisively. "You're not. You're with someone people love to say they saw in person and prove it by taking pictures."

"That's a celebrity," she said.

"No, that's this stupid country that makes people idols and famous even though they've accomplished exactly nothing in their life."

She glanced up at him, wishing the sunglasses didn't deny her the chance to gauge how sincere that bit of self-deprecation really was.

"Oh, and this helps," he said, sliding an arm around her and tucking her tight to his flank. "Stay very close."

"A human shield?"

"No, but I won't get bothered nearly as often when I'm with someone and deep in conversation. When I'm alone, I'm like a walking target."

"Ugh," she said, and not at all because she fit

perfectly under his arm like she belonged there. His body was warm and hard and so, so masculine, and there was absolutely no other way to stay there without sliding her arm around his waist. "That must be a craptastic way to live."

"You can't imagine."

A woman walked by and did a double take at him— not the usual check-out-a-cute-guy double take, either. The woman's step slowed, her eyes narrowed, her mouth dropped to a little O as she reached for her husband to whisper something.

Isn't that Nate Ivory?

Liza could practically read her lips. Nate steered them away with purpose, moving faster, keeping his head low.

"Just keep moving and get into a crowd."

"Holy cow," she murmured as they did. "You really can't go anywhere."

"I can, but I'm selective."

"Like you can't just go to the store and shop like a normal person."

"In some cities, I can. New York, LA are usually safe zones. In some places I lie low, in some I have the stores come to me, and in others, I hire bodyguards."

"Armed?"

He laughed. "Of course."

"Whoa." What would it be like to have to have a bodyguard? What a limiting life that would be and another really good reason for him not to have Dylan.

He guided her to a secluded sitting area between some stores, finding a bench under a tree and choosing the empty side that faced a wall rather than all the people.

"This life would totally suck," she announced as they sat down.

"What sucks is having to be rude to people when I don't want to. I don't want to come off as some kind of cocky asshole, because that does nothing to help my family's image, and really, it's just fodder for tabloids looking for the worst. I don't mind someone knowing who I am, but I hate when I have to be a prick in order to have privacy."

"Well, if anyone bothers you, I'll be a prick for you."

He eyed her up and down. "Sorry. You couldn't if you tried."

"I could be a bitch."

"Doubtful. Now, listen, we need a plan," he said. "I don't want to just wander around here like tourists. I thought we could start by going to my friend's house where I'd been to the party that night, but he's not answering his phone. I left a message, and he knew I was coming."

"Why don't we go to the restaurant where she worked?"

"You know what it is?"

She opened her purse and pulled out her cell phone, where she'd jotted down notes the night before. "I went into the office yesterday afternoon and did some digging around. I know where she worked, the apartment complex where she lived, and the number she gave 'in case of emergency' when she first applied for a job with the County Clerk."

He threw up his hands with a soft laugh. "See what I mean?"

"What? What's wrong with that?"

"Nothing, and that's the point. You're so...efficient.

You're all prepared. You've gone through papers. You have names and addresses."

"That doesn't make me a rocket scientist." She laughed but had to admit the compliment warmed her.

"Maybe not, but it would make you a hell of a right-hand…woman."

"I thought I was going to be the chief unraveler of red tape?"

"You can call yourself CEO if you want." He took the phone and read the notes. "She worked at a place called Red Suns and Hot Buns?"

"We're in Key West, my friend. There are lots of suns and buns."

He just smiled. "Let's go."

Both the restaurant and apartment complex were well within walking distance, so a few minutes later, they were navigating the crowds again, with Nate holding her very close and keeping a running commentary in her ear.

That move easily hid his face from people.

It also sent a million chill bumps over Liza's skin and made her force herself not to turn to him and accidently almost-but-not-quite kiss him again. One woman watched him carefully as they approached, and instantly Nate pulled Liza even closer, pressing his lips against her ear.

"This one's going to be trouble."

"How do you know?"

"Experience. Do *not* make eye contact. That's like an invitation."

Liza sneaked a look at her, taking in the dark hair and bangs, khaki shorts and bright yellow T-shirt. "Nothing about her says trouble," she whispered, but just as they passed her, the woman turned, staring openly.

"Excuse me? Excuse me? Aren't you—"

Nate held up a hand. "Not now."

"But, please, you're Nate—"

"Not now," he said more forcefully, rushing them forward.

"I have to get your picture, oh my God." She spun around, looking behind her. "Karen! Karen, get over here." Her voice rose over the crowd, getting the attention of the closest people.

"Please," Nate ground out. "I'm on vacation."

"So am I!" she replied as if he were making small talk. "Oh my sweet fancy Moses, it *is* you!"

A few more people turned, and Liza could actually feel her own blood start to boil.

"Karen, I need a picture! I have Naughty—"

Liza jumped in front of Nate, right in the woman's face. "Stop it."

The lady drew back, her lip curling. "Who are you?"

"His bodyguard. Back off."

"Liza, you don't have to—"

She shook off Nate's touch and powered closer to the lady, nose to nose with her. "And I'm armed to the hilt and so are ten other people around him that you don't even see right now."

The woman's eyes widened, and she glanced to the side.

"Get the hell away from him, and if you take your phone out for a picture, I will give the signal to shoot."

The other woman sputtered, clearly not sure what to make of a five-foot-four woman making death threats. "I just wanted to…"

Nate put his hand on Liza's shoulder, easing her back. "We're okay now."

The lady looked from one to the other, and Liza stood on her tiptoes and gave the closest thing to a snarl she had in her.

Another woman came running up, breathless, a cup of ice cream in her hand. "What are you screaming about, Joanne? I had to pay for my froyo!"

"That's—"

Liza inched forward. "Don't even think about it."

Joanne held up both her hands, then looked at Nate, her face softening. "Sorry to bother you."

He took Liza's hand and tried to tug her away, but she stayed rooted in the spot, using what she knew was a soul-flattening look to slice the woman down. Finally, the two ladies took off, the others around them lost interest, and Liza slipped back under Nate's arm, both of them rushing through the crowded sidewalk.

He was chuckling, though, tucking her tighter against him. "I was right about you."

"I'm nuts?" She grinned, the rush of adrenaline still pumping through her.

"You're Wonder Woman." He looked down at her, his face so close, but all she could see was her own reflection in his sunglasses. Her eyes were shining, her color high, and her lips parted as if she…

Oh, Lord. Now she wanted to kiss him.

"That was sweet and not necessary and maybe a little dangerous. Don't do it again."

"But I saved you *and* your reputation."

He grazed her cheek with his finger. "You did something else you shouldn't have," he said, his voice low and gruff.

"Lied about being armed? Is that illegal or something?"

87

He laughed softly. "No."

"Then what did I do?"

For a long moment, he didn't answer, then he shook his head, refusing to say.

"What?" she urged. "I don't want to do it again if I did something wrong."

"You didn't do anything wrong." He smiled at her, then dipped his head to plant a soft kiss on her forehead, making the spot burn. "You made me like you even more."

Her whole body betrayed her with a splash of heat and hope she really did not want to feel.

She'd turned him on, damn it. That's what her little spitfire, protective, fearless bodyguard act did. And the next kiss wasn't going to be by accident.

Why the hell did he have to meet this woman under such stupid, complicated circumstances?

"There's the restaurant," she said, pointing to a bright orange sign that promised Red Suns and Hot Buns.

He led them across the street between a break in traffic, slowing down as a horse and carriage full of tourists trotted past. A woman in the back caught a glimpse of Nate. She pointed, then poked her partner, who turned, but the buggy moved too fast, and they darted behind it, into the restaurant.

It was late for lunch and early for dinner, but the outdoor bar was in high gear, with all the stools full and the jukebox wailing some Stevie Nicks. Nate led them to a table near the door, where he pulled out a chair for Liza and took the seat that had him facing inside.

In a few moments, a waitress appeared. A very minimally dressed waitress. She wore cutoff white shorts that revealed a third of her backside and a tight bright red crop top with a sunset emblazoned across her double D's—fake, in his expert opinion. The words Red Suns rolled over her chest, the tops of the letters covered by the ends of her platinum blond hair.

"Whatchya guys havin'?" she asked, shuffling her pad without really looking at them.

"How long have you worked here?" Liza asked.

That got her attention, right on Liza, which is exactly where he suspected she wanted it. If this one got all gooey-eyed over him, they might not learn anything.

"You lookin' for a job?" the girl asked, nodding as if she already knew the answer.

"No, I'm trying to find out about a friend of mine who used to work here, but it was more than five years ago."

"Before my time," she said. "But, hey…" She turned—revealing a matching Hot Buns written across her lukewarm ones—and waved over another server, a dark-haired young woman who looked like she was in her late twenties. "Tracy, c'mere for a sec."

The other woman pivoted on her sneakers and bounced over, a huge, friendly smile in place. "What up, buttercup?"

"You've been here forever, right?"

She rolled brown eyes. "Feels like it. I started in '05." She gave a throaty grunt and dropped her head back. "Why, God? Why can't I get my life together and not be a waitress?" She grinned at her joke. "Who wants to know?"

"This lady is looking for someone named…"

"Carrie Cassidy," Liza said. "Did you know her when she worked here?"

The woman shook her head, frowning as she considered the question. "No, no. I didn't know anybody by that name. When did you say she worked here?"

"About five years ago. I have a picture. Maybe you'd remember her." Liza got her phone, tapped the screen, and showed it to the waitress. "This is her."

The woman leaned closer, and their first server poked her head in to look, too.

"No, I don't…" She squinted and took the phone, staring at it. "Wait, I do know her. She worked here for almost a year. Um." She snapped her fingers, digging for more. "Bonnie? Brandy? What the hell was her name?"

"Bailey?" Nate suggested.

She looked up, face brightening. "Bailey Banks! Yes. I do remember her." She looked at the picture again, thinking, then shaking her head. "Where is she now?"

"Well," Liza said, "I'm sorry to say she died in a car accident."

The woman's mouth dropped open. "No way! Oh my God, I never heard that. She just disappeared after…is that her little boy?" Still holding the phone, she dropped into an empty chair at the table, as if the knowledge that someone she knew had died pressed her down.

"Yes, it is," Liza said.

"That fucking bastard, excuse my French."

Nate leaned forward. "What do you mean?"

She glanced at him, then Liza. "Oh, her dickwad, deadbeat baby daddy."

He saw Liza suck in a breath, clearly unable to speak.

So he did it for her. "Who?" he demanded. "You know him?"

"Oh, hell, everyone knows Jeff Munson around this town. He's been up every skirt in Key West."

"Jeff Munson, the old line cook?" the first waitress asked. "I know him. Whoa, yeah, total manwhore."

Tracy jutted her chin to the picture. "She loved the hell out of him, though. She even moved in with him for a while." Shaking her head, she sighed again. "God, I can't believe she's dead. I wonder if he knows."

So did Nate...what if Liza was all wrong? What if he wasn't anything but a fall guy?

"Do you know where we could find him?" Liza asked.

The other girl stepped closer. "I know where he lives." A soft flush bloomed under her makeup. "I've been there for, you know, after-work parties. It's over in Conch Harbor in those apartment buildings off Twelfth Street."

"Oh, God, no," Tracy said, leaning back and narrowing her eyes at Liza. "Please tell me you are *not* some HRS person who's going to give that kid to Jeff Munson, are you? Because I'm here to tell you, he is *so* not father material. Parties constantly, has a stream of 'ho bags in and out of his place, and hasn't had a legit job in his life. Trust me, he doesn't want a kid to hamper his style."

Nate swallowed, staying very still. She'd just described him.

"No, no, we're not from HRS," Liza assured her. "But it does seem fair to tell him what happened to her."

The waitress shrugged. "He won't care unless it involves money. That dude lives for the next get-rich scheme." She pushed up to get back to work. "Sorry to hear about Bailey. Sweet kid, but maybe not the brightest bulb in the bunch. She was always trying to make him jealous and making up shit about meeting celebrities at work. As if we get Leo DiCaprio in here on a regular basis."

She started to walk away, but Liza reached out her hand and stopped her. "Did she tell you she met Leo DiCaprio?" she asked.

Tracy snorted. "And Ryan Gosling and Adam Levine and, oh my God, that…that billionaire guy, the naughty hottie one from the messy family."

Nate froze—inside and out. To her credit, Liza didn't even blink.

"That girl had a *fertile* imagination and really tried to get Jeff's pants in a bunch over her 'celebrity' encounters, but…" She shrugged. "I just hope she died happy."

"She did," Liza said, her throat tightening. "She was really happy."

"Good, good. 'Cause, man, life is short." She gave a remorseful smile. "I better quit this gig and start living it."

When she walked away, Liza turned to the other waitress. "We're not going to have anything, sorry."

"No biggie. Good luck finding Jeff, and sorry about your friend."

Nate had no idea if she glanced at him, because he looked down at the menu they didn't need and made sure the bill of his cap covered everything but his chin. After a moment, they were alone, and he looked up at Liza, stunned to see her eyes swimming with tears.

"What's wrong?" he asked.

"She probably made you up," she whispered.

"Why would that make you cry?"

She bit her lip, hard, then blinked away the moisture in her eyes. "Maybe she made everything up. Her name, her life, her…everything. What if all those years of friendship were just a lie?"

He reached out a hand, no clue how to console her.

"Come on, Nate," she said, blinking away her emotions. "Let's go find this Munson guy. That place where he lives matches the address for Carrie's last address in Key West. I have a really good idea."

He was starting to know her well enough to know she probably did have an idea, and it probably was good. But something in him, something he really didn't understand, made him hope that this loser guy wasn't Dylan's father. He wasn't sure why he felt that way.

Out of pity for Dylan if that was the case?

Or maybe he was starting to like the idea of Dylan being his?

Chapter Eight

By the time they reached the complex, Liza had fully composed herself, forcing herself to pay attention to the surroundings, avoiding crowds as they walked briskly across town. She could not afford to get emotional about this yet. Not ever.

"All right, we need a plan of action," Nate said as they neared the destination.

"I told you, I have a plan for dealing with him."

"Not alone. Not with some guy who's been described as a douche-bag."

"I can handle a douche-bag. My goal hasn't changed, Nate. I want a signed Termination of Parental Rights so that no one has a claim to Dylan." But that wasn't all, and she had to admit that. "I also want the truth about who he is. Someday, I'm going to have to tell Dylan."

As he nodded, his expression grew darker, maybe realizing just how difficult a conversation that would be, no matter what was said. "That's why you got so worked up in the restaurant."

"This whole situation has me worked up," she confessed. "The sooner I have answers, the better."

"Then let's go." He led her through the open gate to

the Conch Harbor apartment complex, both of them pausing to take in the half-dozen white stucco buildings with beaten barrel tile rooftops.

"This is it," Nate said. "I've been here before."

He was that sure? "Wasn't it dark that night?"

"Pitch, but I came back the next day, remember? I called the limo driver and had him bring me back, but I couldn't find her anywhere, and I even looked through all the mailboxes. No Bailey Banks. And before you ask, no, I didn't go to the apartment manager. I was trying to stay on the down low, but I really did look for her."

Having walked through town with him, she understood. "She was living with this Munson guy," Liza said. "Maybe her name wasn't on the mailboxes."

"Maybe. I know I tried to find her."

"Why did you, anyway? You said she wasn't your type."

He steered her toward the main building, where there was a bank of outdoor mailboxes for every building. "She took pictures," he said after a long beat. "Actually, a video."

Liza almost tripped, stopping cold on the sidewalk to stare at him. "Like of you guys…" She couldn't help making a face. "You mean a *sex tape*?"

He looked away. "I wanted to get it from her before she did anything stupid with it, like send it to the media."

Liza felt her eyes widen. "Did she?"

"The tape never surfaced, and I forgot about it until I saw her picture in that journal. It's not possible you have it, is it?"

"I doubt it. I got rid of all her stuff, and I don't

remember any cameras in her belongings. She used her phone to take pictures."

"Let's hope that camera and what was on it is long destroyed," he said when they reached the mailboxes.

As they started to peruse the residents' names, Liza gathered up the courage to make a simple request. "Listen, if we find him, I have to talk to him alone."

Nate looked up from a row of boxes, frowning. "Why?"

"Because if he sees you, it'll change everything. Who knows how he'll react to you? He won't know me, but he'll know you. I want the truth, and I have the best shot of getting it if I'm alone."

He didn't answer but turned back to the mailboxes. In a few moments, he tapped one. "Got it. J. Munson, unit 335. That's probably building three, third floor, unit five."

"Okay. Wait here for me." She started off, but he snagged her elbow.

"Liza." He turned her. "What's your plan?"

"Besides brilliant?" She gave him her most dazzling smile. "I'm going to dangle money in front of him."

He slid his sunglasses off, his look stern. "Let me assure you from personal experience, that is not a smart thing to do. A blackmailer never goes away, ever. They get their teeth in you and will suck you dry."

"Blackmail?" She laughed softly. "I'm so much more creative than that." She tried to ease her arm out of his grasp, but he held tight. "What is it, Nate?"

"I don't know," he admitted. "But…" He swallowed and took a slow breath. "I guess I was starting to get used to the idea."

"Of Dylan? You'd be disappointed if Dylan wasn't

yours?" She couldn't keep the shock out of her voice. "I'd think you'd jump for joy."

A little war waged behind his eyes, tawny brown darkening to something deeper and quite powerful. "I don't like the idea of you going up to this guy's apartment alone."

But that wasn't what was bothering him, was it? She didn't want to argue, though. "Then stay close by but out of sight. I'll text you if I'm in trouble." She managed to slip out of his grasp, but he got her other shoulder and pulled her close.

For a moment, she was certain he was going to kiss her. She stayed still, looking at him, waiting for it, but he just shook his head. "Be careful."

"I will be." She stepped away and darted toward building three, not turning but knowing Nate wasn't far behind. Up the open stairs that led to each floor, Liza tried to forget him and remember the plan she'd hatched when they were talking with the waitress. She'd gotten enough clues about this guy to feel certain this would work.

At the top landing, a sign pointed left to units four and five, so she turned the corner, following the wall on her left and the railing open to the courtyard below on her right. She rounded the bend, smacking right into a man hustling the other way.

"Oh, shit, damn." Papers—mail, it looked like—went flying, along with more curses.

"I'm so sorry," Liza said, as the man bent over to grab some envelopes. "Really, sorry."

She helped, glancing at the return address as she scooped up what had fluttered away. *J.B. Munson*. Bingo. And with a middle initial to add credibility, too.

Glancing at him from behind a lock of hair that covered her eyes, she got an eyeful of hair and tattoos and faded khakis hanging off sun-weathered skin.

"My bad, sir," she said, straightening and smiling innocently.

He nodded, finally seeing her. And giving her a chance to see his face and any resemblance to Dylan. Brown eyes, yes, and maybe the mouth, but…

She realized he was checking her out, too. "We forgive pretty girls around here. Apartment policy."

"Thanks and, um, listen, you wouldn't happen to know where I could find a Mr. Jeffrey B. Munson, do you?"

He frowned slightly, shaking back some long, streaked hair. "You're looking at him. Why?"

"Really? That's fortunate." She slipped her hand into the side pocket of her purse where she kept her business cards and handed him one. "My name is Liza Lemanski, and I work for the County Clerk in Collier County as head of the public records department, and we've been looking for you."

"County Clerk. Shit." He refused the card, all friendliness gone. "Parking ticket? Moving violation? Don't tell me I owe freaking back taxes, lady. Call my lawyer."

"None of the above, sir. A deceased citizen of Collier County has named you a beneficiary in her will, and we have to complete some paperwork and identification in order to expedite the payment."

His eyes widened. "Seriously? How much?"

She gave him a tight, professional smile. "Most people usually ask the name of the deceased."

"Oh, yeah." He brushed back some hair. "Who

croaked? Aunt Thelma from…I don't know where the hell Collier County is."

"The woman's name was…" She took a chance. "Bailey Banks."

His jaw unhinged, color draining from his face. "She's dead?"

At least there was a hint of remorse in his tone, but if this was going to work, there had to be none in hers. "I'm afraid so, and her estate attorney is trying to locate all of the beneficiaries to get copies of the will, but you—"

"How did she die?"

No emotion, Liza. None. "I believe it was a car accident. And it was instant." Oh, why did she add that? A county courier wouldn't know that. "Anyway, I have a few questions for you, and then we'll get the paperwork mailed out."

He looked at her, but she could tell he was thinking about Carrie—Bailey—and not her questions. Which made it a good time to ask them.

"Can you confirm the date she left Key West?"

He frowned, pulled back to the moment, maybe not smart enough to wonder why that question would matter to an estate attorney. She hoped.

"Um, I'd have to check something—no, no. Of course I know. It was my birthday, well the day after. We'd had a party, and shit got pretty real, you know, and she didn't like it. She just…took off."

"And that day was…"

"June 13, however many years ago. Four? Five? I guess five years ago."

Exactly the week Carrie had come into the County Clerk's office. They'd always celebrated June 20 as their "friend anniversary." She tilted her chin up, willing herself not to show any reaction.

"And she was alone when she left?"

"Yeah, as far as I…well, yeah. Sort of." He looked away for a second, his wiry frame tense.

"Mr. Munson? Was she alone?"

He blew out a breath. "More or less."

"What does that mean?"

"Well, listen…" He threaded his fingers though his hair, then kept his palm on his unshaved face, rubbing it while he looked at her. "Does that will really call her Bailey Banks?"

The way he asked the question made perfect sense if he knew her real name. And Liza had seen her Social Security card. She knew her friend's legal name. "Actually, that's what we call an aka. Her legal name was Careen Cassidy, but they are one and the same."

He nodded, all doubt erased from his features as if she'd given him a verbal password and could be trusted. "Yeah, she liked to use that Bailey name. She thought it sounded prettier or…" He shook his head slowly as the facts hit him. "But, wow, so she died. Man, that's sad."

"Very."

"Did she, um, have any other beneficiaries in that will?"

Just Dylan, her *son*. She hedged her bets with a nonanswer. "Her parents passed away."

"I know that. I went to their funeral."

Did he? Because Carrie's journal said Nate had accompanied her there. *Oh, Carrie, why did you leave behind this mess? Why couldn't you tell me the truth?* "Then who do you mean?"

"Like, did she have any…a kid?" He croaked the last word.

"I'm not at liberty to say, Mr. Munson. Why do you need to know?"

"Because…" Another puff of air, this one loud and slow. "'Cause when she left…" He looked to the side, embarrassed. "She was pregnant."

Here we go. She took a wee breath of fortitude and looked him straight in the eye. "Are you the father?" she asked bluntly, willing every muscle in her face to stay in the act of impartial third party and not someone who loved that child with her whole heart.

"Well, technically, yeah, but…"

"Technically? You are or you aren't, sir." Her heart punched her ribs so hard it had to be leaving bruises.

"Would it change me getting any money?" he asked. "I mean, I hate to be crass and all, but we did some…you know…paperwork."

A slow heat rose up from her belly, threatening her stability. "What kind of paperwork, Mr. Munson?"

"I signed a piece of paper. Something called a terminal…rights termination or—"

"Termination of Parental Rights?"

"You know what that is?"

"I do." He'd signed a TPR already? "And if you could just show me a copy of that paper, Mr. Munson, and your legal ID, then I can"—*adopt Dylan*—"get on my way. Do you have it?"

"Somewhere. How much money do I get?"

Nothing. "As a courier, I'm not given that information, but an attorney will contact you after I get a picture of that form. Can I see it?" Please, *please.*

"Yeah, yeah. Gimme a sec." He turned and walked a

few feet to the door of unit five. "Just wait out here. The place is a hellhole."

"Okay." She crossed her arms and leaned against the railing, looking out to the courtyard and fountain below. All the while, she willed her heart rate to slow and the questions to stop. She had plenty of time to ask questions…like *why*? Why had Carrie worried about his father, or his father's "powerful family," taking Dylan if she'd already had that signed paper? Carrie had known who the father was all along, but…why was she scared of "his family" coming to take him?

"Beneficiary of a will?" The whisper made her gasp and step back to see Nate hiding around the corner. "That's good, Wonder Woman."

"What are you doing here?" she mouthed.

"*He's* the father?" He sounded purely disgusted.

Liza felt the same way but couldn't deal with those thoughts right now. She had to get that paper.

"I guess I'll know in a minute. Get out of here."

The door clicked, and she flashed a look at Nate and used her fingers to zip her mouth in warning. When she turned, she saw Jeff coming down the hall holding a legal-size document.

She hustled forward to meet him, praying Nate stayed out of sight.

"I can't believe I found this, but here you go."

Forcing her hand to be steady, she reached for the document, recognizing it instantly, along with the authentic seal of the State of Florida. She touched legal papers like this a hundred times a week and knew this was the real deal.

The *signed* real deal.

"Hang on," she said, grabbing her phone. Aware of

his gaze on her, she channeled her inner professional. "If you'll just hold that for me so I can get a picture, Mr. Munson, I'll be on my way."

"I signed it because I was pissed at her," he mumbled.

She clicked a photo of the signatures on the top page, not answering.

"But I still, you know, cared about her."

She snapped the midsection full of legalese, the most important part. "I'm sure you did, Mr. Munson."

"She was just so messed up, living in a dream world half the time, writing these ridiculous stories about meeting movie stars and shit." His voice rose with frustration. "It was so stupid. She thought she was going to be some kind of famous author, and she made up these stories. Once she even…"

She lowered the camera and met his gaze. "Once she even what?"

"She liked to make up stuff that would make me jealous. And when that didn't work, then she'd…do stuff to make me jealous."

Like sleep with famous billionaires in limousines. "Such as?" she prodded, hoping he didn't realize that no one in her position would ever ask that question.

"She cheated on me," he said gruffly. "And made sure I knew it."

She had to ask. *Had* to. "Then how are you absolutely certain this child"—she tapped the paper he held—"is really yours?"

"Oh, I'm certain of that," he said.

"How?"

He snorted. "You think I'd sign a paper without knowing?"

She gave him another quick, professional smile and tucked her phone away. "Well, thank you, Mr. Munson."

"So, you sure you don't know how much I get?"

"I honestly don't know." She took a step back, ready to end the conversation, but he came with her.

"Wanna have a drink to celebrate?"

"Celebrate?" Was he serious? "A woman is dead. A woman who you say was the mother of your child. What's to celebrate?"

All that doubt came back into his eyes as they narrowed at her. "Who the hell did you say you were again? What's your name?" Doubt shifted to something more menacing.

"My name—"

"Give me your card." He came too close, right in her face, forcing her back. He didn't stop, inches from her now, slowly lifting a hand as if he was going to grab her.

"I told you I'm with the county."

"Where's this will? Where's your proof?" He slammed a hand on her shoulder, squeezing. "Who are you, lady?"

"I'm with the—"

"Back off!" Nate shot forward from around the corner, reaching the man in three long strides, shoving him off Liza. "Get away from her."

The legal document fluttered into the air.

Jeff's eyes flashed, fear for a second, then anger. "What the hell is going on here? Who are you?"

"Just leave her alone or—"

"You can't have that picture." Jeff lunged at Liza. "Gimme your phone!"

Nate knocked him away, but Jeff reached out and got in a swing. He missed the punch, but rocked Nate's sunglasses halfway over his face and flipped his baseball cap off his head.

"Nate!" Liza shrieked.

Stumbling backward, Jeff sputtered in shock, his long hair caught between his lips.

"Let's go, Liza," Nate said, scooping up his hat but keeping his eyes on Jeff.

The other man stared at him, chest heaving, eyes squinting. "Wait a second."

Nate pulled Liza closer. "Let's go."

With no hesitation, he guided her away, fast, almost running, but Jeff flew forward again, throwing his whole body on Nate to try to pull him to the ground. Nate swung around to shake him off, but the guy gave a fight.

Liza stepped back, hands to her mouth, watching in horror as Nate lifted the smaller man off him and slammed him against the wall.

"Don't make me hurt you." Nate ground out the words, lifting the other man a few inches off the ground.

"I know you!" Jeff's face was red, his eyes furious as he stared at Nate. "You're in the tape! You're the one! You're the guy Bailey fu—"

"Shut up." Nate shook him, veins popping in his neck with the effort to hold the guy still.

"No," he said. "No, I won't shut up. I know everything. I know everything."

Very slowly, Nate released his grip on the guy's shoulders, taking one step backward. "Leave us alone," he said. "We don't have any more business here."

"I got shit on you, man. I got shit." His feet hit the floor, but Jeff shook his head with an ugly smile. "I could do some damage, too."

Nate held out his hands in something remotely

resembling a truce. "Just let it go, pal. No harm, no foul."

"Or you could give me some cash for my trouble."

Nate's whole body visibly bristled. "Shut up."

"I can." He brushed his T-shirt, confidence building again. "For a fee."

Nate leaned right back into his face. "What part of 'shut up' don't you understand?"

He shrugged. "Say, ten grand."

Nate puffed a breath of pure repugnance, stepping farther away. "Scum."

"What did you call me?"

Liza and Nate shared a look and silent agreement. Wordlessly, they started walking.

"What did you call me, you dickhead?"

"Just keep going," Nate whispered under his breath, a hand on her back to usher her forward.

"'Cause I can make your life a living hell!"

"Move," he ordered, nearly breaking into a jog just as Jeff fired his parting shot.

"You'll pay, motherfucker! You will pay for what you did to me!"

Chapter Nine

Liza didn't breathe easy until Nate snagged them a cab and they were finally off the streets of Key West, headed back to the yacht. But as the taxi made its way through a warren of palm-lined streets with pastel houses and coconut palms, Nate stayed stone silent.

"I'm sorry," she said to break the uncomfortable quiet.

He didn't answer, his jaw clenched as he stared out the window.

"I feel like now I have what I want"—she patted her phone, safely tucked into her bag—"and you have a big fat problem."

He still didn't reply, making her heart sink.

"And I'm still in shock that I could be such a poor judge of character, because Carrie fooled me. I mean, she did have a great imagination. I used to laugh at the bedtime stories she made up for Dylan…"

He swallowed, visibly fighting some inner demons.

Liza took a chance and put her hand on his thigh. "I wish you'd talk to me."

When he turned, the fury and frustration in his eyes

107

were clear. "If he has that tape, he'll release it now."

"You can't be sure of that. First of all, that's a big if from five years ago. Second, what does he have to gain?"

He snorted. "Revenge."

"If he wanted revenge on you for sleeping with his girlfriend, he'd have sold that tape years ago."

"We stirred a hornet's nest."

And Nate got stung. "Will it make you feel better if I say I'll take the job?"

He almost smiled. "Yeah. We're a good team."

"I outsmart them and then you beat the crap out of them?"

"I didn't beat the crap out of him," he said with a dry laugh, the first in hours. "I could have. Should have. You did outsmart him, though, with the whole beneficiary of the will thing." He put his hand over hers, the tender touch surprising her. "I'm glad you have what you wanted from the very beginning."

She studied the angles of his jaw and strong cheekbones, the warmth in his eyes, and the softness of his mouth. Without consciously thinking about it, she inched slightly closer. "The cost was high."

"Don't worry, I won't pay him."

"What if there's a sex tape released? Isn't that exactly the kind of thing you're trying to get away from? Won't that set you back with your family, and your grandfather, the Colonel?"

"He won't like it," he acknowledged, his tone showing just how much of an understatement that was. "And it won't help the image of the new baseball team, especially now when we're still looking for investors so we don't have to sink so much of our money into it.

Yeah, it would suck all around. Especially if it somehow has Dylan's name attached to it."

"I doubt it will, but I appreciate you thinking about that aspect." She lifted their joined hands, surprising both of them by bringing his knuckles to her lips. "And fighting to protect me."

He turned his hand so he could cup her jaw. "You're worth protecting." He rubbed his thumb lightly, grazing her skin. "And I'm reminded once again how little I'm worth."

She rolled her eyes, giving her head a shake of disbelief.

"And I don't mean money," he said. "Just the shit that is my past."

"At the risk of sounding like a page from a self-help book, Nate, you are not the sum total of your past. People change. Look at Carrie. Whatever she was in Key West, she showed up in my office contrite and reformed. I loved her for what I thought she was. Finding out that she had a messy past and a nasty boyfriend and a weakness for rich playboys doesn't make me love her less. She changed."

"I bet you helped her and didn't even realize it."

The compliment, even in the face of the other sweet things he was saying, squeezed a band around her chest. "I don't know," she admitted. "I wish she hadn't felt it necessary to lie to me."

"Maybe she thought you'd judge her. I know I..." His voice trailed off.

"You know you what?"

He smiled, finally releasing her jaw but still holding her hand. "When I come face to face with someone like you, it's humbling."

Was he serious? "Nate, I am the most unremarkable person alive. I work in the County Clerk's office. I live with my mom. I drive a Ford Focus with sixty thousand miles on it. The last thing I am is humbling to a..a..." Did she have to say it again? He was a gorgeous, famous *billionaire*. "A person like you."

"You should see yourself the way I see you." He searched her eyes, as close as he could get without kissing her. "You're resourceful. You're caring. You're beautiful. You're...*damn*."

Damn? Damn *what*? She waited, but the list had come to an end. "Um, don't stop now."

He smiled and gently brought his mouth to hers, the first contact featherlight, almost making her shudder at the sweetness of it.

He sighed into the kiss, adding some pressure but still showing incredible restraint.

"Bottom line, Liza." He broke the kiss just as the cab pulled into the harbor. "You're too damn good for me."

She inched back, trying—and failing—to wrap her head around that statement. But there were so many levels of confounding. Like the fact that he even thought about her in terms of...him.

Unless... "You mean for the job you're offering?"

"No. For me."

After he situated Liza in his sister's favorite stateroom and showed her that she had everything she needed to shower, relax, and change for dinner once they were underway for the return trip, Nate retreated to his own suite to think.

Except, somewhere in Key West, he'd stopped *thinking* and started *feeling*. Feeling something he was not familiar with: inadequacy.

No woman ever made him feel that way. Of course, he'd spent his life with women who were exactly like he was—cocky, arrogant, draped in the trappings of wealth, which covered a multitude of sins.

Sins that he so badly wanted to erase. So what did this little sojourn down to the Keys do? Magnify them. Increase the likelihood of more of those transgressions coming to light. Make him even more ashamed of how he'd lived, what he'd done, and what stupid, dumb decisions he'd made in the past.

When Liza saw that sex tape—which he had no doubt that little prick would find and sell to the highest bidder—she'd be disgusted by him. And for the love of all that was holy, he did not understand why that bothered him so much, but it did.

Almost as much as what he had to do next. But he had no choice. There was a way of doing things in his family—the Ivory way—and he knew exactly what had to be done. Scandals, problems, issues, and any kind of thing the Colonel called "whitewater" had to be dealt with inside so they presented a unified front to the outside. There was no getting around that.

Even just dialing the number made him feel better, getting this off his chest, and into the hands of a person who would know what to do.

The butler answered the phone, as he always had and always would. "Colonel and Mrs. Ivory's residence, how may I assist you?"

"Greetings, Emile. It's Nate."

"Hello, Mr. Ivory. How can I direct your call?"

"I need to speak with the Colonel, please. Is he available?"

"Let me check, sir."

Of course, the old man kept him on hold for nearly three minutes, giving Nate enough time to rehearse what he was going to say. How he'd cushion the blow and try to minimize the damage control.

God knew, it wasn't the first time they'd had a call like this.

But he so badly wanted it to be the last.

"Did you change your mind? Are you coming to dinner tomorrow night?"

Nate sighed into the phone, and all his cushioning and control evaporated. With the Colonel, there was only the truth. "I got a problem, sir. I need to give you a heads-up on something."

He heard the grunt of disgust and disapproval on the other end. Or maybe that was the old man settling into his leather chair, bracing for his grandson's latest debacle. Either way, Nate told him everything. Including his deep-seated suspicions that Jeff Munson might not be telling the truth…about *anything*.

Liza turned in front of the full-length mirror in a walk-in closet the size of her bedroom at home and admired the final results. She might feel like she didn't belong in the queen's velvet and marble stateroom, but she had to admit, she looked the part.

Of course, there were no "everyday" clothes to be found. No simple skirt or T-shirt or casual white pants. And almost everything looked brand new, some still bearing a silk ribbon with a designer's name signed in ink.

Which meant…the closet was full of original couture.

The least-formal thing she found was a sleeveless white sundress that fell to her ankles in soft waves of linen and lace, fitting a little tightly in the bodice, but loose over her hips and waist. She'd dipped into the cosmetics drawer in the bathroom, applying some makeup to accentuate her eyes because…well, face it, because Nate obviously liked her eyes.

In fact, based on that kiss in the cab, he liked more than that.

The thought stilled her, making her nibble on her lip and consider what that meant. It meant a dizzying amount of female hormones rushed through her, which was pathetic but undeniable. And it meant that—

"Liza?"

The tap on her stateroom door made her abandon her thoughts to pad barefoot across the creamy carpet to open the door. And somehow manage not too swoon.

"A tux?"

He grinned. "For dinner on *N'Vidrio* with a gorgeous woman?"

"You look"—*unfairly hot*—"formal."

"I'm sure I'll take the jacket off and lose the tie after dinner." He stepped back and took a moment to look her up and down, smiling in approval. "You're stunning, Liza."

Self-conscious, she brushed the soft fabric. "Please

thank your sister for letting me borrow her dress." She leaned forward to playfully whisper, "I think it was made expressly for her."

"Then it's a shame you look better in it. In fact, keep it. She'll never miss it, and you look amazing."

Liza held out her bare foot. "We don't wear the same size shoe, and I couldn't bear to ruin this pretty dress with those sandals I had on all day. I feel a little...underdressed."

"No need." He toed off the black loafers he wore and slipped off his socks to reveal his own bare feet. Which were as ridiculously attractive as the rest of him. *Oh, Liza. This is bad.*

"Now we're even." He kicked the shoes into the room, then took her hand, tucking her closer.

"You feeling okay?" he asked as they followed a teak-floored hallway to the other side of the yacht.

"I'm fine," she said. "How about you?"

He gave her a wide, unexpected smile. "I'm really good."

"Not worried anymore?"

He lifted a shoulder. "What does worry get me? I'd rather enjoy this trip home with you. Here we go."

He opened the door to a private dining room with a small table set for two surrounded by rich mahogany and gleaming glass and about fifty flickering candles all around the room.

"At the risk of repeating myself...wow."

"This is where I eat when I'm alone."

She glanced up at him. "And how often is that?"

"Lately? More often than you think. Come on and enjoy the view."

The sliding doors were open to a spacious side deck,

114

looking right out to the sea. The sun had set, leaving the sky a haunting shade of violet and the water near-black. The longer she looked up, the more stars she saw in the heavens, along with a nearly full moon that bathed them in soft white light.

"Pretty romantic setting," she mused as they walked to the railing.

"I have it on good authority that it'll be raining in a few hours, so we should take advantage of the clear skies. What would you like to drink?"

"Surprise me."

He stepped away and picked up a phone in the dining room, spoke softly, then came back outside, standing right behind her.

"I want to ask you a question, Liza." His voice was low and close to her ear, giving her chills.

"Okay."

He ran his hands up her bare arms. "Are you cold?"

"No. Is that the question?"

He laughed softly. "No." With his hands on her shoulders, he slowly turned her from the stunning view to face him. Which was another stunning view. "Are you satisfied with what we found out today?"

She frowned. "Satisfied?"

"Do you believe that I'm not Dylan's father?"

"Yes," she said. "After thinking about it for the past two hours, I believe that Carrie must have had one hell of an imagination and maybe tried to make her boyfriend jealous or...I don't know. Don't you?"

"I want to put it behind us."

Us. The word made her whole body feel light. "So I can work for you and this issue won't always be there?" Because surely that's what he meant.

"Yeah," he agreed. "And so when I kiss you tonight, you won't be thinking about my past, especially with her."

She didn't know what made her dizzier—the fact that he was going to kiss her or the fact that he had no doubt he was going to kiss her. She lifted a brow. "Will you?"

"Kiss you or think about her?" He pulled her closer. "I'll answer one of those questions easily." He kissed her on the mouth, a steady, strong, serious kiss that was somehow different from what they'd shared in the cab.

"Nate?" she whispered into his mouth.

"Hmm?"

"Is kissing you going to be part of this job you're offering?"

"Actually, we have a strict kissing-is-allowed policy, so..." He kissed her on the nose, lightly. "Yes."

Before she could answer, a steward tapped on the dining room door. "Hold that thought," Nate said, stepping away.

She leaned on the railing, facing the twilight sky and navy blue water, her lips still tingling from the contact. Her whole body, in fact, was humming pretty hard from her head down to her bare toes.

Nate came up behind her again, reaching around to offer a crystal martini glass with clear liquid. With the dimming light behind it, she could see every cut in the glass, which refracted the light like a diamond.

"Another house special?" she asked.

"Just a simple dry martini, but the glass is a family secret."

She took the drink, a little surprised at how heavy the

crystal was. "I thought Ivory Glass was the tempered stuff that went into skyscrapers."

He gestured toward a wide leather sofa. "That's true and certainly how my grandfather made the fortune. But we also have some very small and exclusive lines of glass and crystal that are really more for personal use and to give as gifts. There's actual diamond dust blown into the glass." He toasted her. "And you may keep yours."

She laughed. "Thank you. It's like I get to keep everything I touch on this yacht." Except him. She couldn't keep him. She had to remember that all this was a dreamy fantasy, and not reality. Not Liza Lemanski's reality, anyway.

"Cheers." He tapped her glass and sipped, holding her gaze over the rim.

"You seem much more relaxed than when we left town," she observed without taking her own drink.

"I am. I talked to my grandfather."

She inched back in surprise. "You did? You told him…about the tape?"

He nodded. "It's how we roll in the family. No surprises, no matter how bad they might be."

"What did he say?"

He blew out a slow breath. "Some choice words, but, you know…"

"No," she admitted. "I don't know."

"He knows my history and believes in my future."

She smiled, the words a lovely echo of what she'd told him earlier. "Yes. I like that. I do, too."

He leaned closer and kissed her lightly. "You haven't tasted the house special yet."

She answered by intensifying the kiss. Parting her

lips, she let their tongues touch, tasting lemon and dry vermouth and the sweetness of a man who'd finally come to terms with his demons.

"I just did," she whispered into the kiss. "And he tastes great."

Chapter Ten

All the parties, all the women, all the noise and chaos and music and wasted nights on this yacht, and Nate simply couldn't remember one night he enjoyed more than his dinner date with Liza Lemanski.

Fresh off the best and most honest conversation he'd had in years—maybe ever—with his grandfather, Nate's mood soared as they laughed, held hands, sipped martinis, and talked about everything and nothing until the twilight turned to complete darkness.

Eventually, they moved into the dining room for lobster and salad, chocolate mousse and dessert wine. With the rain still holding off, and the sea breeze warm and strong, they took a long walk around the deck. The stewards and staff did exactly what he paid them to do—disappeared when he wanted them to—adding to the sensation that they were utterly alone, which was all he wanted to be.

They reached the upper deck with not a soul in sight. He guided her to the oversized leather sun bed at the far end of the yacht.

"We must be getting close to Naples," she said,

eyeing the distant lights of the mainland on the port side. "If I see lights, we've passed the Everglades."

"We are, but there's no reason to dock tonight if you want to stay at sea."

"I have a reason. His name is Dylan." She gave him a light elbow. "Trust me, kids change everything."

"I trust you." He ushered her to the sun bed, moving a few tufted pillows to make room for both of them. "But we still have time for a dip in the pool or drink in the spa if you like."

"Hmm." She considered that as she settled next to him, letting him snuggle her under his arm. Her body fit perfectly against his, curvy and soft and feminine. He already itched to touch more skin, to feel her under him and on top of him. He satisfied himself with stroking her bare arm and watching her eyes shutter closed, telling him she wanted the same thing. "I'd have to borrow a bathing suit from your sister."

"Or…not."

She laughed softly. "Don't tell me. You have a strict skinny-dipping-for-all policy that you personally enforce for every employee of your new company."

"I like the way you think, Ms. Lemanski. Ideas like that will have you promoted in no time."

"Promoted to what?"

Very slowly, very carefully, he tucked his arms under her and eased her on top of him. "Over me." Perfect. Her slender legs slid right over his, her hips slipping right where he wanted her.

"Is that my promotion or position?"

"Both."

As she settled against his chest, he was only slightly surprised to feel her heart beat steady and strong and a little fast. He stroked her back, up and down, sliding into the dip of her waist, then inching over the rise of her backside, getting the tiniest whimper in response.

Pressing a kiss on her hair, inhaling the sweet floral scent of her, he let his hips rock once. She looked down at him, nibbling that lower lip.

"So what's the company policy on making out?" she asked.

"Not required, but always…encouraged."

She smiled and offered her mouth, their first kiss warm and full of promise. When it ended, she pulled back and looked into his eyes. "Don't you have more questions about my qualifications and background?"

"Your qualifications are obvious—you proved yourself in the field today. Background?" He considered what he really wanted to know about her. "Yeah. Why don't you have a boyfriend?"

"What makes you think I don't?"

"You're here on this lounge with me. You're not the type of girl to do that if you were involved with someone."

She smiled. "So true. Well, I'm involved with a guy who stands forty inches tall and has a weakness for chocolate milk and purple dinosaurs. What's your excuse?"

"Honestly? I can't commit, have questionable taste, and don't trust anyone who might be after things other than true love."

The response made her bow her back as she lifted her body in surprise. "Really? Is all of that true?"

More or less. "I have to be careful, for obvious reasons. And I have been known to choose unwisely when it comes to women. And commitment? Let's just say it's eluded me. I haven't met the right girl yet."

"I understand. I haven't met the right guy yet."

He brushed some hairs off her face and took another long trip in the beauty of her eyes. What would it be like to be the "right guy" for a woman like her? "So where does that leave us, Liza?"

"Us? I guess…boss and employee?"

"Nothing more?"

She gave him a slow smile. "What exactly are you suggesting?"

"I'd like…to know you better. Nothing official, nothing committed, just better."

She drew in a breath, regarding him. "In other words…almost-not-quite anything."

"Depends on your perspective."

"Right now," she whispered, closing her eyes, "I feel like I'm too close to have perspective."

"But close enough for this." He pulled her in for a long, slow, deep kiss, sliding his tongue between her lips to part them. Her body felt boneless and limp in his arms, sweet and soft and womanly as she intensified the kiss. Their legs meshed, their hips rocked, and their mouths began exploring everything they could taste.

Blood thrummed hot in his veins, swelling him against her, making him move in a natural rhythm that she met with each strained breath.

He moved his hands up and down her back, one settling on the lovely curve of her backside, the other tunneling into silky hair. He angled her head and curled one leg around hers, somehow making them fit as though they were made for each other.

She tasted like chocolate and peppermint; smelled like roses and salt air, and felt like…heaven.

"You're as good at this as everything else," he whispered, tipping her chin up so he could plant tiny kisses on her throat.

"Not from too much experience," she said. "Certainly not with billionaires on megayachts."

"I don't want to be a billionaire on a megayacht."

She laughed. "Hate to break the bad news, but you am what you am, baby."

But he wanted to be more. Different. Better. "Forget that, Liza," he whispered gruffly.

She answered with a slight whimper when he found a sweet spot right above her collarbone.

"Forget who and what I was," he whispered.

"Naughty Nate?" she teased. "How could I?"

"I hate that name." His voice was thick with repugnance.

"Then don't be...naughty." She kissed his mouth, his cheek, his forehead and went back to his mouth for more, making it impossible for him to be anything but.

His hand touched her warm, smooth thigh, lightly stroking her skin, sending another explosion of response through his already electrified body.

"Kiss me again, Liza."

She did, arching her back, giving him the chance to plant kisses on her throat and in the V-neck of the dress, inhaling the feminine scent and licking the delicious skin. Unable to resist, he dragged one hand up her side and curled around to brush her breast, getting a soft sigh of pleasure in response.

And a splat of rain on his face. And another hit his hand where it rested on her thigh.

"There's the rain," she said, turning to look up at the charcoal sky, the moon well hidden by thick clouds. "I guess Mother Nature's giving us a message. Time to stop."

"Here's what I say to Mother Nature." He reached down to the side of the chaise, patting the leather for the button. "There we go."

A low electric hum preceded the awning, which rose from behind them, as if by magic. Liza lifted her head to follow the navy blue canvas as it flattened out over them.

"Are you kidding me?" She laughed.

"We're on a sun bed, Liza. Sometimes people want shade. Or rain protection."

She sat up, straddling him, the white skirt bunched around her thighs, her hair falling back as she looked up at the awning in wonder. "That is...oh my God, *so cool*."

She looked beautiful in the newly formed shadows, her hair tumbling over her shoulders, a smile of pure joy across her face, her slender body wrapped around him.

"You hiding any other tricks, Nate?"

"Well, in case there are any mosquitoes..." He pressed the second button on the panel below him, and sheer gauze netting rolled down from all four sides.

That got another sweet squeal of delight. "Amazing!"

"So are you," he said gruffly, reaching up to pull her down against him, then eased her on her side so they were lined up on the sun bed.

For a few minutes, they stayed very still, looking at each other in the dim light, the steady drumbeat of the rain matching the one in his chest as he let himself be transfixed by her.

A breeze fluttered the netting, making her shudder.

"Are you cold?"

She shook her head. "I'm scared."

"Of what? I promise, I swear..." He lifted one hand as if to show her how safe he was. "We can lie here and listen to the rain. I promise, I'm good."

She closed her eyes as if the words physically affected her. "Yes, you are. You're so..." She searched for a word, clearly frustrated. "You're not going to like this."

He lifted a little from the headrest, concerned. "Tell me anyway."

"You're not naughty."

He snorted softly. "Stupid word, but tell that to the rest of the world. Anyway, I earned it."

"Well, you're not anymore. Not with me. Not now. Not most of the time. You're...nice."

That made him laugh. "First time I've ever been called that. But I guess you bring out the nice in me." Which was weird. "I don't know why or how."

She smiled. "It's okay to be nice. And it's okay to be..." She rolled a little closer, snuggling into him and looking up. "A little not nice, too."

He took the cue and kissed her, slow and soft and, oh, hell, not *nice*. He plunged his tongue and curled it around hers, coaxing a moan from her throat.

"Nice and deep," he whispered between breaths.

She melted into him. "Very nice."

He stroked her side, lightly brushing her breast with his thumb. "Nice and tender." He barely touched her but felt her harden under his thumb.

Dipping his head, he suckled her jaw and throat, kissing his way to her earlobe, licking it. "Nice and wet."

"Ohhh." Her sigh was pure pleasure, the sound and

125

feel of it on his cheek making his whole body tense.

He flicked his tongue all the way down her throat and over her breastbone, suckling her skin for a taste. He filled his hands with her curves, dragging them over her hips to carefully gather her skirt, inching it up so he could touch her skin.

When his hand pressed her taut thigh, she eased her body back on top of his, as if neither one of them could resist the temptation to press against each other.

"Nice and..." He slid his hand higher and higher, their hips rolling in rhythm as he reached the dip where her cheek met her thigh. "Sweet."

"Mmm. Nate..."

He stilled his hand. "Too nice for you?"

She looked up at him, chaos in her eyes. "I'm dying here."

He curled his hand around her bare behind, finding the silky string of a thong, tracing the line of it right...between...her...legs. She was soft and slippery, making him hard and hot.

"Too nice," she whispered. "So nice. Oh my God, Nate, don't stop."

He wouldn't. Turning her for a better position, he looked at her all mussed from his hands, her lips pink from his kisses. Her eyes lost all their blue-green to the dark, dark promise of arousal. "Let me, Liza. Let me show you how nice I can be. Let me..."

She nodded, her breath coming so hard and fast now, she couldn't talk. He wanted to see what pleasure did to her. He wanted to give her everything and take nothing. He didn't stop to analyze that but caressed her and kissed her with all the tenderness and passion he had.

She let out a tiny cry, jerking once into his hand, then biting her lip as she looked at him.

"Come on, Wonder Woman," he urged. The rain drummed harder overhead, loud enough to drown out her sweet moans of gratification, strong enough to wrap them in a cocoon of water and silk and secret, stolen kisses.

"Nate..." She shuddered again, gripping his arms, digging her fingers into his muscles as he slid his finger all the way into her, stroking the wet, warm skin, finally teasing an orgasm from her quivering, out-of-control body.

It took a minute for her to catch her breath and release her grip, long enough for him to quell his own arousal because he knew—he just knew—they weren't going any further.

"Okay," she finally whispered. "I'll do it."

Or maybe they were going further? "You will?" He couldn't stop the smile. "I'd have been willing to wait, but..."

"I'll work for you."

He blinked, surprise and disappointment colliding. Then he laughed, rocking into her so she could feel how hard that disappointment was. "Probably a good time to make your salary demands, too."

"I only have one demand."

At her serious tone, his smile evaporated. "Yeah?"

"Well, two. Dylan can be in the children's program at the resort."

"Done. Easy. What else?"

"We can't...I can't..." She closed her eyes. "This sounds really selfish considering the pleasure you just gave me, but I'm not ready for...everything."

He didn't answer right away, waiting to hear if there would be a time limit on that one. There wasn't.

"Ever?" He wanted to show restraint, and had, but if they worked together, that might be impossible.

She sighed and cupped her hand on his jaw. "I need some time to forget some things."

"Things in your past?"

"No, yours."

He frowned, then figured out what she meant. "Carrie?"

"I can't fall into bed with a guy she…" She shook her head. "I have to know you for you, not the man she made up in that journal, not the guy in the media, and not what I thought you were. Who you really are. And then…"

So he had one more person to prove his worth to. "I like that plan. Start Monday. The sooner you know me, the sooner we'll finish what we just started."

She smiled, kissing him and wrapping her arms around his neck. "Will do, boss. Now hold me and tell me something I don't know about you."

He cuddled her closer, smoothing her dress and adjusting himself to let the desire abate. "Something you don't know about me. Let me think."

"And it can't be anything that I'd read in the paper. A secret."

"Okay." He pressed a kiss on her head and confessed, "I've never done that before."

She looked up at him, eyes wide. "You're lying."

"No, I'm not. I've never completely given someone…that. Not without expecting everything in return."

She smiled slowly. "You're right. I bring out the nice in you."

Holding that thought, they stayed under the awning until the rain showers passed, kissing, whispcring, laughing, sharing secrets and, finally, sleeping in each other's arms until the yacht docked in Naples and they had to say good night.

Chapter Eleven

Liza put the caller on hold and looked over at Nate, lying on the sofa, one leg bent, his head propped on his arm, reading a legal document he had resting on his chest. It would be so easy to climb over the desk that separated them and cuddle up next to him and do what they both wanted to do ever since they set up a temporary office in Acacia, the spacious beachfront villa he'd taken over for the business.

So far, they'd resisted. But…

Heat, familiar and constant and always strong, curled through her at the thought. Of course, she said the only thing she could. "Nate, it's the county commissioner's office on line one."

He turned his head to smile at her. "Calling to say the agenda is finalized?"

"And to invite you to attend the meeting as an honored guest."

"Probably to thank me for the donation of forty-six new live oak trees for the Naples Parks and Rec Department." He rolled up, still grinning at her. "Genius idea, Wonder Woman."

She angled her head, still not quite used to his

compliments on her work, even though he'd been doling them out for almost three weeks. "Hey, you wrote the check."

"But the gesture got us slipped into the County Commissioners' meeting three months ahead of schedule."

"I know county weaknesses, it's true." She shrugged, indicating the flashing light on the phone bank. "Take the call, do your thing, and when you're done we can go over the access-road permits."

He wiggled his eyebrows playfully. "The fun never ends."

She laughed. "This *is* fun. Aren't you having fun?"

He leaned closer. "There's a beach twenty yards away, a pool in the back of this villa, and a bed the size of a small country in the master suite. All screaming for *fun*."

"Hey. We have a deal." She pointed a finger at his face.

"And I've been upholding my end of that deal for twenty days…and nights."

The fact that he counted did crazy, stupid things to her insides. The wait was nearly over, and she knew it. Longing looks, purposeful touches, and a couple of smoking-hot kisses after-hours and Liza was fairly certain where this "work relationship" was headed.

And she couldn't think of a single reason not to say yes. "Access-road permits are fun."

"Okay," he relented. "And then?"

And then she'd have to pick up Dylan after the children's program ended. Sighing, she glanced at the clock on her desk. "Take the call, Nate, before they shove us clear into the June meeting."

He didn't move, staring so hard it felt like he could see right through to her soul. "You know that middle color in the rainbow?"

She tried to come up with a quip but failed, shaking her head instead, no clue where this was going, only that it would be...*nice.*

"That kind of magical mix of turquoise and emerald, not quite one, not the other, but still precious and inviting?" He almost closed the space between them, inches away now, the soapy, masculine scent of him tormenting her.

"Yeah?" she managed.

"That's the color of your eyes." Closer still. "I could look at them for hours."

She closed them for a second, almost unable to take the assault when he flirted like that. Was he teasing? Was he serious? Three weeks into the job, and she still couldn't tell. Nor could she even remember the mundane and dreary existence that was the County Clerk's office.

Still, she dug for the professionalism he so loved to tear away. "Take the call, Nate. And remember the county commissioner is named Sandra Hutchings, and she has an inflated ego, a tiny attention span, and a fiery temper."

"Good to know. God, I'd be lost without you."

She laughed. "Oh, and she would like to have her picture with you in *The Mimosa Times.* Don't keep her waiting."

"I won't." When he turned into the hall to go to the master suite he used to take calls, he stopped and looked back at her. "No one likes to wait too long." With a wink, he disappeared.

For a moment, she rested her chin on her hands,

staring at a half-dozen stacks of papers and two neatly arranged files, all labeled and sorted and ready to be tackled. A sensation of pure satisfaction rolled over her. She *loved* this job. And she...loved...okay, she was pretty damn *fond* of her boss, too.

Taking their attraction to each other up a notch—or *six*—wasn't a matter of *if*, it was a matter of *when*. And where...and how. Oh, she knew how. She'd fantasized about how every day and night since they'd docked his yacht in Naples. First, they'd—

The soft hum of an electric golf cart and the sweet sound of Dylan's laughter pulled her from her reverie. Having him so close by during the day was certainly a blessing...and a curse. She was never sure when he'd be cruising by on some seashell-gathering adventure or field trip to the gardens. Still, a smile she couldn't hide broke across her face as she rose from her desk to go to the door.

Late afternoon sunshine poured in, warming her as much as the sight of the boy she loved dearly.

"Aunt Liza!" He practically tumbled out of the cart, followed by his platinum-blond best buddy, Edward Browning. Eddie's mother, Tessa, the resort gardener, was at the wheel, climbing down with one hand on a slightly distended belly.

They'd met a few times—enough to know Tessa was the glowingest pregnant woman in history.

"We come bearing requests," Tessa said in greeting.

"S-L-E-E-P!" Dylan spelled, jumping up and down. He wanted to go to sleep?

"O-V-E-R!" cried his little friend.

Liza laughed, mostly at their high-fiving on the spelling, coming around to greet Tessa. "What's this about?" she asked.

Tessa's dark eyes danced as she eyed the two boys. "They've cooked up an idea, but we need your permission."

"A sleepover?" Her skepticism must have been evident because Dylan immediately jumped into a "Please, Aunt Liza" litany that Edward joined until they were both shushed. "You've never gone to a sleepover," she said to Dylan.

"And I've never hosted one," Tessa admitted. "But Emma's been invited to a birthday party, so I'm down one child and these two…" She smiled at the boys, shaking her head. "They are inseparable. My husband and I don't live far, in town, and I assure you we'll have them in the sack by eight—"

A chorus of "awws" interrupted her.

"Or nine," she added with a laugh. "But we'll take care of him, I promise."

"I'm not worried about his care, it's just…" She put her hand on Dylan's head. "It's a first for him."

"We'll make it special."

"Okay—"

"Woo hoo!" Dylan and Edward were jumping again, but that wasn't enough celebration, so they started running in circles around the golf cart.

"What's all the ruckus out here?" They all turned to see Nate standing in the doorway, trying to look stern, but a smile grew as he watched the whirling dervishes. Dylan came to an instant stop, his face brightening like he'd been handed two scoops of ice cream.

"N-A-T-E!" He tore toward Nate, arms outstretched, getting hoisted in the air upon arrival. "I'm going to my first sleepover!"

"You are?" He made a surprised face, then looked

over Dylan's shoulder to Liza, his expression changing from surprise to something else. Something that made her whole body tingle in anticipation. "Then we'll have to…"

Have a sleepover, too?

He lowered Dylan to the ground. "Make sure you have a great time."

Her heart tumbled around because she knew he was thinking of the great time they'd have. "And maybe I can take your Aunt Liza out for dinner," he added.

They hadn't had dinner since the night on the yacht, and she'd kind of ached for another night like that. But Nate had been following the rules and her lead since the day she started working for him.

"Oh, you should get a reservation at Junonia tonight," Tessa said, referring to the resort's fine restaurant, run by her chef husband. "Ian's special tonight is veal chops, and they're to die for. And sweet potatoes right from my garden."

"Perfect. It's a date." Nate ruffled Dylan's hair, but his eyes were hot on Liza. "As soon as we finish the access-road permits."

When he went back inside, Tessa's smile was amused and all-knowing. Were they that obvious?

"This is perfect," Tessa said.

"Completely," Liza agreed, barely aware that her voice held a sigh of dreaminess to it.

"So the rumor mill is true," Tessa mused. "There's more than Bucks business going on in Acacia."

Liza felt her cheeks warm. "No, no…he's my boss." She glanced at the closed door. "We just work together."

Tessa laughed brightly. "That's what I thought about

Ian at one time, too. Now I love his children as my own, and we have another on the way."

Liza drew back, surprised. "Edward and Emma are…"

"Ian's from a previous marriage, but they're all mine now. And this one on the way." She rubbed her belly, and her eyes twinkled. "I'm living proof that anything is possible. In fact, here on Barefoot Bay, we're starting to think *everything* is possible."

Was it? Could normal, ordinary, not-quite-anything-special Liza Lemanski win the heart of a world-famous billionaire who'd already stolen hers? "That's a lovely sentiment."

"It's true!" she insisted and leaned closer to whisper, "And it's obvious he has feelings for you."

"It is?" She felt like an eighth-grade girl, but the only person she had to discuss this with was her mother, who couldn't see straight on the subject of Nathaniel Ivory. She'd practically embroidered the towels with their adjoining initials already.

Tessa started to round up the boys but took a moment to continue the girl talk. "He seems like a really nice guy in person. Nothing like his public image."

"He is different from what you'd expect."

"I know you're not asking for it, but my advice? Don't fight whatever's in the air down here. Sometimes the most unlikely people make a great team."

A great team. Nate called them that at least twice a day. Could they be? Right now, they were almost…quite…not anything official. But something told Liza that was about to change.

After they exchanged phone numbers and Liza kissed Dylan a few dozen times, they drove off, with the two boys sitting on the back of the golf cart, waving like lunatics. Liza stood and watched them rumble away.

"Hey, Wonder Woman."

A shiver of anticipation worked its way through her body at the low and sexy tone of his voice. She didn't turn, instead taking a steadying breath and trying to consciously hold the moment in her hand. "Yeah?"

"It's time."

Yes, it was. Very slowly, she turned to see him standing in the doorway, holding up some papers. "Access permits."

Smiling, she took a few steps closer, holding his smoldering gaze, aware of each pulse beat in her throat, each strained breath, each spark of electricity arcing through the air.

"Access"—she took the papers with one hand and pressed his chest with the other, pushing him back into the villa—"no longer denied."

He answered with a slow, deep, hungry kiss as she let the papers flutter to the floor.

"It's about time," Nate murmured into the kiss that had them both breathless in under a minute. Liza didn't answer, tunneling her hands into his hair and gripping his head to press their lips harder.

She heard Nate kick the door closed and then inhaled sharply when he backed her right into the mahogany frame, blocking her with a body that was as hard as the door behind her.

"You're not going to wait for a dinner date, are you?" she asked with a half laugh.

"Oh, we'll have dinner. Later." He pinned her arms over her head with one hand, annihilating her mouth and throat with hot kisses. "Much later."

He already had her sweater halfway up her torso.

"Nate. Here?" If he hadn't been holding her, she'd have probably melted to the floor.

"Anywhere you want." He got the sweater over her head, tossing it to the side and making her laugh. But nothing was funny to him. His face was raw intensity, his hands already all over her breasts, his erection slamming mightily into her stomach, making her want to...ride.

"C'mon." Still kissing and unsnapping her bra, he walked her across the room, flipping lace and satin strips in the air.

He stopped, holding her back to look at her half-naked body, his eyes shuttering as he took her in. "Gorgeous. *Gorgeous.*"

She tried to laugh, but the chill of desire and air-conditioning made her quiver and reach for his warmth. "We're never going to make it to the bedroom."

"Not this time." He closed his hand over her bare breast, dipping his head to kiss and lick, and she automatically bowed her back to offer him everything, dizzy and disoriented. He stepped her backward, and her backside hit a piece of furniture. Some papers shifted. The stapler fell. And the next thing she knew, he had her flat on her desk.

A pile of file folders dumped to the ground. "Oh, there went the capital expenditures analysis." She bit her lip and rolled against the crazy hardness of him.

138

He sat up enough to unbutton his shirt and flatten her with another fierce look. "Sorry." He shook off his shirt, his broad chest heaving with the next breath.

"No, you're not."

He flashed a grin and rocked his hips against her, then came back down for more kissing, more touching and exploring, and something slammed to the floor. "And the zoning surveys hit the dirt."

Laughing, he unzipped her jeans. "As they should. Take these off, Liza."

She lifted her hips and let him help her slide them down, his head following the route so he could kiss her belly. Squirming on the desk, she gripped his shoulders, digging her fingers in and lifting her head to enjoy the view of him nibbling at her panties.

He looked up and caught her eye.

"Careful," she said, nodding to the last pile of folders next to his legs. "The investor presentation handouts are about to eat it."

He didn't look away as he pulled her panties down her thighs. "So am I." He practically growled the sexy promise.

She fought a scream when his tongue slid into her, making her flatten both hands on the desk and send her to-do list flying.

She didn't care. The only thing she had to do was…this. Pleasure careened through her, tightening every muscle and firing every nerve ending. Her fingernails dug into her desk blotter as she rose to meet every stroke of his tongue, fast and furious, then slow and deep.

Suddenly, he stood, making her open her eyes in a panic. He couldn't stop. But he was yanking off his jeans, pushing down a pair of boxer-briefs and, oh…my.

She pushed herself up to appreciate the sight of his manhood. Opening her mouth to speak, she stared. And ached for him—*all* of him—inside her.

"Nate," she finally whispered, reaching to touch him. "I want you."

"You got me." Before she could close her fist over him, he slapped his hands on the desk, forcing her back again. "I mean that."

Falling back, ignoring a pen cap that jabbed her shoulder blade and the ring of the phone a few inches from her head, she stared up at him, absolutely certain there was more to that statement than sex.

"You got me," he repeated, coming closer like he was going to kiss her. But he inched to the side and put his mouth right over her ear. "You got my attention." His breath tickled and teased. "You got my interest. And, Liza, sweetheart, you got my heart."

The phone went silent, and so did her head. No quips, no jokes, no comebacks. She had his heart?

Neither one of them moved, despite the heat of his hard-on throbbing between her legs, the stickiness of bare chests pressed against each other, and the matching drumbeats in their chests.

"What are you saying?" she finally asked, her voice little more than air.

"I'm saying…" He lifted up enough to look at her. "That this isn't…" He struggled for the word, and she didn't begin to try and fill in the blanks. "That this is…" He swallowed, searching her eyes, holding her gaze. "That we are…"

Finally, she smiled. "I get it. We're a good team."

He closed his eyes and returned to the safer place

next to her ear, denying her the chance to appreciate the raw honesty in his eyes. "You make me a better man, Liza."

She closed her eyes against the sting.

"Nate, I…" *Love you.* Could she admit that now? Was it the kiss of death or—

"Open the door! I know you're in there!"

They both bolted upright at the shock of intrusion, Liza letting out a little cry of surprise.

Who could that be? One of his friends? Someone on staff? Who would—

A fist—or something wooden—smacked against the door, and the handle jiggled furiously. "Open up, Nathaniel Ivory! I have the DNA tests!"

What? Liza put both hands over her mouth. Jeff Munson? Was he here to make good on his promise to hurt Nate? Fear and confusion collided, nearly blinding her as she blinked in shock.

"Holy shit," Nate muttered, leaping off her and frantically looking for clothes in the mess.

Liza rolled off the desk, smashing her hands over her breasts in case whoever it was broke down the door, because they sounded mad enough to do just that.

"Let me in!"

"All right, all right!" Nate hollered. "Hang on."

"Who is it?" she demanded, scooping up his shirt to slide her arms into it for protection. "What is he talking about?"

He looked at her, and for the first time, she noticed he'd gone pale…and silent.

"Who is it, Nate?"

"My grandfather." He stepped into his jeans and gave her a nudge. "Go hide in the bedroom."

Her jaw dropped so hard it nearly hit her chest. "Your—"

"I will shoot the damn lock, young man."

"Go! You don't want to meet him like this."

No, she didn't. But... "Did he say he has the—"

"Liza!" He barked the word, stunning her into silence. "Go back there."

She froze, vaguely aware of the door handle shaking hard again but fully aware that she stood naked but for Nate's shirt over her shoulders.

"Please," he added. "This might get ugly."

Get ugly? It was already pretty damn unattractive from where she stood. Closing her eyes, she pivoted, stepped over a sea of papers and underwear, then walked around the corner to the bedroom, her head buzzing and her heart still slamming her chest.

But she didn't close the door. Instead, she stood stone still and listened as Nate opened the door.

"What are you doing here?"

"Demanding to take what is mine." It was easy to hear now that it was the voice of a much-older man, accompanied by heavy, uneven footsteps into the room. She cringed, thinking about what he saw. How would she ever—

"Where is he?"

She put her hand on the doorjamb, frowning. *Where is who?*

"Listen, Colonel—"

"No, you listen to me. You were right to send me that test. One hundred percent right. That boy is an Ivory through and through, and there is only one thing to do. We take him home, son. Damn the torpedoes! We take him home."

All around her, the world grew darker, shakier, and completely airless. What was he saying? What was he…

The question faded, replaced by the obvious answer. Nothing made sense. *Nothing*. Except her worst fears had been realized.

The Ivory family was going to take Dylan away from her.

Chapter Twelve

"*What?*" It was the best Nate could manage under the circumstances. The intrusion, the news, the plummet from a sexual high to a disaster. "What the hell are you talking about?"

The Colonel powered into the room, waving his cane like a scepter, his steel-gray eyes taking in the hot mess, then settling on Nate's barely dressed state. "You call this work?"

"I call it...*private*." Which was unheard of in the Colonel's eyes. "What do you mean that boy is an Ivory?"

"You called it!" he bellowed, leaning heavily on his cane as he looked down at a jumble of papers. And clothes. He used the end of the cane to lift a pale pink bra by one strap and let it dangle in front of Nate's face. "Is this what you call being a changed man?"

Nate closed his eyes and ignored the taunt. "Please tell me what you found out." Except, he already knew. He'd known when he impulsively sent the DNA kit Liza had left on his smaller boat up to his grandfather for private testing.

When he left Jeff Munson in Key West, he simply

hadn't been as satisfied with the man's signed paper. He'd tried to put it out of his mind, but every time he saw Dylan, he wondered. Sending the DNA test to his grandfather was really to prove the truth to both of them, since the Colonel had already talked about forcing the issue himself.

"I found a match right down to the cell matter, son. This young man is part of our family, and we will raise him as ours."

Oh, God. His? Dylan was *his*.

Nate stole a glance over his shoulder. He couldn't see the bedroom door from where he stood. Could Liza hear this whole conversation? Would she come barreling out here any minute to fight tooth and nail for the child she considered her own?

Even though that child was *his*?

Nate stabbed his fingers into his hair, swiping it back with a deep sigh. "Look, Colonel, I will handle this."

"Like hell you will." Using his cane, he flipped the bra into the air, sending it flying to land on Liza's desk.

Nate bristled, swamped by frustration, compounded by an intense and unfamiliar coldness. Because he'd been yanked from sex with a woman he deeply cared about? Or was his grandfather's disapproval leaving Nate cold?

"I will handle it," he repeated, keeping his tone low and calm. "Liza has full guardianship—"

"Pay her off, get her signature, and..." He looked around, surveying the oversized living room that doubled as a main office. "Where is the boy? I thought he was on the premises."

"He's not here. And you can't pay a person for her child, like—"

145

"He's *not* her child." The older man pounded his cane, drawing his bushy eyebrows together, deepening the crevice between his eyes. "Nathaniel, you can pay a person for anything, and you know it. She'll have a price. When can I see him? I'd like a look at him and so would Mimsy. She's resting right next door at the little villa called Saffron. Nice place, by the way. I like this re—"

"No, you can't." He ground out the words, the effort to balance his seething temper with a lifetime of compliance to everything this man wanted. "You can't give someone money and expect them to accept that in exchange for a living, breathing child."

"Nathaniel." The Colonel's tone showed he knew what kind of battle was brewing inside his grandson. "I'm disappointed in you."

Nate waited for the words to hit their target and make him feel like a failure. But that sensation didn't take hold in his heart. Something else did.

A deep, profound, wholly alien feeling that made him want to protect, defend, and support Liza Lemanski...over *anyone*, including the Colonel.

"I don't care if you're disappointed in me." The words surprised him as much as his grandfather.

An old gray eyebrow launched north, rising above silver-rimmed glasses. "Excuse me?"

"I don't," he said, the reality picking up steam inside him. "I don't care if you withhold your almighty approval or tie up your purse strings or cut me off from family dinners on Sunday night. *I don't care.*"

The words were so liberating, he almost laughed out loud.

"Did you hear that?" Nate asked, raising his voice so

someone not in the room had to hear it. "I don't care what you say or do or threaten, *Grandfather*, because I will not let you hurt Liza or have her...my"—*our*— "son."

"I hear you," the Colonel said, pushing himself off the cane. "And, by the way, a young man from Key West sent me a package in the mail. I was going to throw it away, but I think it might be of interest to some of the private investors you're trying to interest in this little baseball project of yours."

His jaw dropped as he stared at a man he thought he loved, a man he thought ruled a family with a velvet fist. But what he saw was a man he didn't want to be like at all.

"I'm not afraid of a scandal, Colonel," he said. "But I will fight to the death if you try to take Dylan from Liza." He swallowed. "And me."

"I wouldn't care if you wanted to raise him, but"—he waved the cane over the chaos of papers and clothes— "you are clearly not the changed man you claim to be, and I would worry for the boy."

"I don't need your worry or your care." Nate closed his eyes and took a deep breath. "I really don't need your approval. So, if you don't mind, you can leave now."

The Colonel stared him down, eyes narrowed, jaw clenched. "Nathaniel, I—"

"You can leave now."

A slow, sly smile pulled at the older man's face as he made his way across the room to the door, his slightly lame gait more pronounced than Nate remembered.. "Well, son of a bitch, I never thought I'd see the day."

"What day?" he asked. "The day I really changed?"

The Colonel put his hand on the door and opened it,

standing to face the sunshine for a brief moment. "The day you fell in love."

Maybe they both happened on the same day.

The Colonel stepped outside, and Nate opened his mouth to argue, then shut it again, along with the door. Inside, alone, Nate stood for one second, letting the adrenaline dump through him.

Holy hell, he'd stood up to his grandfather, and won. He'd broken that debilitating need for the Colonel's approval, and he could breathe. He'd proved to Liza what he'd been trying to tell her: that he really was a better man.

Hadn't she heard?

He turned, expecting her to come darting out of the hall, eyes bright with pride, arms extended, her heart soaring like his was. Now they would make love. And talk about Dylan and how they would...

But all he heard was silence.

"Liza?" He walked toward the bedroom, his pulse ratcheting up. "Liza, did you hear that?"

He stepped into the room to see the sliding glass doors that led to the back wide open, the sheer curtain fluttering with the beach breeze.

She hadn't heard enough of it, because she was gone.

Liza darted across the Casa Blanca parking lot, clutching the too-large sweat pants she'd found draped over a chair in the bedroom. Nate's shirt was buttoned all wrong, so the right side of the collar kept tapping her in the chin, and stones and shells jabbed her bare feet as she ran toward the sanctuary of her little blue Ford Focus. She shouldered her bag, eternally grateful she'd been in the habit of hanging it in the bedroom closet. Who knew she'd have to make an emergency getaway out the back door one day?

Twenty more feet. Just twenty more feet and—

"Liza!"

She froze, recognizing Nate's voice even from across the resort property. Fisting her hands with a grunt, she used everything she had not to turn and look and melt and forgive. Because what he'd done was unforgivable.

"Liza, wait!"

She powered on to her car, already digging in her bag for keys.

"Liza, damn it, don't leave!"

With one hand on the door handle and one grasping the sweats that were threatening to eliminate any possible chance of a dignified escape, she turned toward the sound of his voice. He was running full-out, still bare-chested and wearing jeans and no shoes.

He seemed to move in slow motion, calling her name, holding out his hand, desperation pouring out of him.

"Liza, please wait." He slowed down when he got close enough to stop yelling, catching his breath from the sprint.

She shook her head and held up one hand. "Don't, Nate. Don't come at me with explanations and rationalization. You lied to me. You went behind my back and had that test done. And you called in your biggest artillery to get what you want." She squared her shoulders and pointed her finger at his face. "You think some rich old Marine and his brood are going to take my child away from me?"

He let out a slow breath, his chest rising and falling. "He's my child."

Anger and fear ricocheted through her as she whipped all the way around. "You bastard! You would play that card?"

"I'm not playing anything, and I'm not a bastard." He tunneled his fingers into his hair, shoving it back. "I had to know."

"And not share that with me?"

"I had to know," he repeated, his voice taut. "I was going to tell you the test results."

"But you decided it made more sense to bring your grandfather in and, in fact, to have him control the test, which really makes me question its validity and…and…*why* would you do that?" She nearly sobbed out the question, but it didn't matter. She was hurt and confused and furious and sick at heart. No use trying to hide all that.

"Because my family always comes first. Always *came* first," he corrected. "That's how it is, that's how we stay together."

"No, that's how you all stay under the control of one old man who has fed the monster with billions of dollars." She huffed out a breath. "What did you do, send him the swab I gave you?"

His only answer was a pained expression. "I thought—"

"I don't care what you thought!" she fired back. "You could have told me. You could have trusted me. You could have"—*not made me care about you*—"shown your true colors and been an asshole for the last three weeks."

"I *have* trusted you. And I have shown my true

colors." With each word, he came closer, rounding the last car in the lot that separated them. She backed into her car, not wanting the assault of his apologies or kisses or that big bare chest that covered a black heart.

"How long did you stay and listen to that conversation?" he asked.

"When he asked for Dylan, I left. Oh, maybe I heard the part about paying me off." She choked her sarcasm. "From the king of 'we never pay anyone to get what we want.'"

"You should have stayed longer. I sent him away."

"Well, he'll be back. No doubt with a legion of lawyers and a bottomless checkbook."

"I made him leave, and I won't let him use lawyers or dollars or anything to hurt you. I won't," he insisted. "Not you and not Dylan. I swear."

She regarded him for a long time, mesmerized by the pain and sincerity in his eyes. "I've seen that look, Nate. That same look in your eyes."

"What look?"

"The one that says you're real and you mean this."

"I am, and I do." Encouraged, he closed the space between them, inches away now. "When did you see that look?"

She tipped her head. "Back there, in the villa."

"Because that was real, and I meant what I said."

"And you were five seconds and two inches from fu—"

He put his finger on her lips, silencing the ugly word. "No."

"Um, *yes*." She jerked to the side to escape the burn of his touch, but it didn't work. Her lips were still warm. "Unless you want to give it another name, Nate. All I

151

was about to be was another girl. A notch on your bedpost. Or desk. Or...*limo*."

He flinched, and she waited for a jolt of satisfaction, but felt nothing like it. Only sadness.

"You're wrong," he said. "I know what it looks like on the surface, but you're as wrong as my grandfather for making assumptions about me. I wish you would give me a chance." He reached out his hand, palm up, the peace offering obvious.

If only she could. "Your family is never going away."

"And neither is the fact that Dylan is my son, but," he added quickly when he saw the look on her face, "you are his mother in every other way. And that, Liza Lemanski..." He leaned forward and whispered in her ear, "Makes us family, too."

Her chest squeezed so hard she didn't bother trying to breathe. Instead, she reached into her purse and pulled out her keys, turning to the car. Without saying a word, she opened the door and slid into the driver's seat.

After she turned on the ignition, she tried to pull the door closed, but he held it open. So she looked up at him, right into his eyes.

"You have to answer one question," she said.

"Anything."

"Which family matters more to you?"

He hesitated one second. Just one millisecond, and she knew the answer. Getting a hold of the door, she yanked it closed with a loud bang and backed out of the parking lot to go get Dylan.

They'd been so close. So, so close to...love. Almost-but-not-quite love.

Chapter Thirteen

Nate put his signature on the final document and checked the clock. He still had twenty minutes to finish before Zeke and Becker showed up and another ten before the reporter came.

Grabbing the next file from the pile, he opened to find all the documents labeled and in chronological order. He pushed thoughts of the woman who'd made his life so organized out of his mind. She'd been gone long enough that he knew he had to find another assistant, but he still clung to the hope that every time that door opened, she'd be standing there, blue-green eyes sparkling, both arms out bearing his second chance.

A knock kindled life into that hope, but the sound of his friends' laughter crushed it out. He got up to let them in, checking the time once more.

"We have twenty minutes," he said to Zeke and Becker when he opened the door. "And I need every one of them to get my work finished. Why don't you guys wait on the beach?"

Zeke and Becker did simultaneous double takes at each other.

"I'm sorry," Becker said. "I thought we came to Nate Ivory's villa, not a workaholic's. Who are you?"

"I'm running a damn operation that you're both deeply invested in, so I'd think even a moron like you, Becker, would want me to work."

Becker muscled into the villa. "Give it up and get a damn assistant."

Zeke stayed in the doorway, slightly more sympathetic. "No word from her yet?"

He shook his head. "But my grandfather has completely backed off, so there's that victory." A hard-won battle, too, keeping the old man from tracking down Dylan and demanding to take him away. But the Colonel finally let go and returned to the Ivory Tower with Mimsy.

Behind him, Becker slapped a friendly hand on Nate's shoulder. "You know what you need?"

What he needed was the smart, gorgeous, sexy, amazing woman who was raising his son. "I don't drink when I'm working," he replied. "Which is pretty much twenty hours a day now. But the good news is we can have a groundbreaking very soon."

"That is good news," Zeke said, finally coming in.

"I didn't mean you need booze," Becker finished, undeterred. "You need a grand gesture."

Nate laughed. "I know you like those."

"Not about what I like, my man. This is about exactly how to tell a woman you love her."

He inched out of Becker's touch. "How grand?"

"The bigger the gesture, the harder they fall is my experience." He grinned at Zeke. "And in Mr. Nicholas's, too, if I recall from his not-too-distant past."

"He's right," Zeke said. "You have to show her you

mean business. Do something she isn't expecting. Get her attention and keep it."

As the two men settled onto seats in the living room, Nate returned to his chair at the desk that took up most of the middle of the room.

"I bet you can't wait to get out of this villa and into an office on-site," Zeke said.

Nate shrugged. The villa—and this desk, including all the files—was still a connection to Liza. She knew where he was in case she wanted to—

"Hello? Anyone in there?" A woman's voice accompanied a light knock on the door, and Nate hated that his heart actually skipped a freaking beat. But that wasn't Liza.

"She's early," Nate said. "My calendar says noon."

Zeke was already up, shooting him a look. "You better have an attitude adjustment for this interview," he said, keeping his voice low. "I know *The Mimosa Times* isn't *The New York Times*, but we have to make the entire island love us and support this baseball team and stadium. Cultivating a relationship with a local reporter is critical."

"Plus, maybe she'll be hot," Becker—the *moron*—suggested. "And you can hire her to replace the nice girl you scared away."

Nate gave him the finger right before Zeke opened the door. "Ms. Simpson?"

"Yes, hi. I'm Julia Simpson from *The Mimosa Times*."

Becker was right, damn it. She was quite attractive, with long blond hair pulled into a neat clip and cheekbones from here to Sunday. "I know I'm early, but I'm..." She laughed softly. "I'm really

155

excited about interviewing you three for the feature."

She was introduced all around, taking a minute to get their names straight, and let out a few nervous laughs before she accepted a cold glass of water and perched on the edge of a chair. She crossed long, shapely legs at the ankle and daintily tucked them as she opened her notebook on her lap.

Nate tried to see her as the beautiful young woman she was, probably a week out of journalism school and deliciously adventurous in…

No. He wasn't interested in other women. He wanted the one he'd had and lost. The one he'd loved and—

"Would that be possible?" Julia asked breathlessly.

He'd missed the question completely, damn it.

Both of his friends looked at him expectantly. Shit, a business question. Of course, he was off in the clouds thinking about Liza.

"I know it's asking a lot," she said. "But I really have to have something exclusive and different. I need an angle that no one else is going to have about this project. Something that will show our readers and your new neighbors exactly what you guys are made of."

Zeke leaned forward. "We could let you see the blueprints for the owners' box. It's going to be top-notch."

She made a face, clearly not interested in blueprints.

"A sneak peek at some of the ballplayers we're recruiting?" Becker suggested.

"Um, well, the team's a long way off. I was thinking of something about you guys. Something personal." She shifted her gaze to land on Nate. "Your life makes good, you know, publicity." Those angular bones deepened with a blush. "It might be fun to get a little bit deeper in the head of 'Naughty Nate.'"

Becker snorted softly, and Zeke actually laughed, but Nate had a little white light pop inside the very head she wanted to get into. He put his hands on the desk and nodded, unable to fight a smile.

"Honey, I've got a story that will sell newspapers, go viral, and skyrocket your career."

Her eyes lit up. "Really?"

Next to her, Becker sat up straighter, his own grin wide as he pointed to Nate. "Now, that's what I'm talking about, Ivory. Grand. Perfectly *grand*."

"Excuse me, ma'am, but your little boy…"

Liza whipped around, almost dropping the oversized paper towel package she held when she spied Dylan leaning far out of the shopping cart to pull a stream of about six hundred deli numbers out of the dispenser a foot away.

"Oh!" She tossed the paper towels into the basket and lunged for the five-foot-long trail of paper. "Dylan. No."

"Here, I got that." A man came up next to her, snagging the tickets out of Dylan's grasp.

"Thank you." She looked up at him, meeting a kind smile and friendly blue eyes behind serious horn-rimmed glasses. "I'm really…thank you."

He flipped off the top of the dispenser and spun the wheel so all the numbers rolled right back into place.

"Whee!" Dylan cried out, delighted.

"Tough to shop with kids," he said, maintaining eye contact with every word. "I try to get here before I pick mine up at day care."

"Oh…" He picked up his own kid at day care and did the grocery shopping. Single? "Yeah, it's a challenge," she said, giving her own smile, even though the whole exchange felt foreign and forced.

"I'm Mike." He offered his hand, and she barely touched it, not surprised that contact with a light pole would have conducted more electricity.

"Hi, Mike. Thanks again."

Dylan saved her by reaching for the number roll again. "Whoops, I better get him out of here. Bye." She pushed the cart quickly away, feeling bad about dissing the fine-looking and hopeful man, but he wasn't…

He wasn't Nate.

Blowing out a breath of self-disgust, Liza maneuvered the cart into the express line, absently placing milk and cereal and bananas on the conveyer belt. How long was she going to moon over the guy, and worry…he'd come and claim his son?

So far, for a few weeks anyway, he'd let her be. She'd received a paycheck in the mail after a week, and, thankfully, she got her crappy job back at the County Clerk's office. And every single night, after an evening of bearing pitying looks from her mother, she'd cried herself to sleep, longing for—

"N-A-T-E!"

Oh, God. "Shhh." She closed her hands over Dylan's tiny shoulders and gave his head a kiss. Even he missed Nate.

"N-A-T-E!" He pointed to the right, kicking his legs.

Liza's heart rolled around her chest as she looked

toward the door, expecting, hoping, *dreaming* her man would be charging into Publix to save her from a lonely, boring, single existence. Or maybe to take Dylan.

But there was no—

"N-A-T-E!" Dylan started kicking again, and finally Liza followed his finger to the rack of tabloids next to the checkout.

And this time her rolling heart fell into her stomach with a thud. The headline blurred for a moment, forcing her to blink to make sense of it.

Naughty Nate Officially Off The Market: Eligible Billionaire Has Fallen In Love

"What?" She reached her hands out, her gaze moving to a picture of Nate taken right outside the villa, leaning on the wall, arms crossed—so of course his biceps looked huge—a serious look on his face.

"That sound you hear?" The voice came from right behind her, forcing her to glance over her shoulder and see the man named Mike behind her in line. "A million hopeful hearts breaking in pieces."

"Including mine," said the woman behind him. "One less eligible billionaire for us to dream about."

Slowly, Liza pulled the brightly colored newspaper from the rack, and Dylan's squeals reached a higher pitch as Nate's face got closer.

"N-A-T-E! Nate!"

Behind her, Mike cracked up. "Sounds like your son knows your guilty pleasures, Mom."

She barely smiled, trying to muster up the concentration to read the first paragraph, but nothing would come together like a noun, verb, or sentence. Just snippets and phrases like *hit by a lightning bolt* and *love at first sight* and *she brings out the best in me.*

159

"Who?" she demanded, giving the paper a shake.

Mike laughed some more, clearly amused by her frustration. "No wonder I struck out," he said. "Your bar is too high."

The nosy woman behind him poked her head into the conversation. "The whole story broke in a local paper over on Mimosa Key. And they say one of the tabloids had some old sex tape, but this announcement trumped that news, and they didn't even run it."

"I read that," said the woman right in front of Liza, scooping up the bag of groceries she'd just finished paying for. "She's his administrative assistant. Talk about winning the love lottery!"

Liza stared at the paper again, heat and hope and something she'd never ever felt before exploding in her chest, making every cell feel…alive.

"You know he's living over there in Barefoot Bay," the checker chimed in as she started ringing up Liza's bananas. "In fact, my aunt's going to the baseball groundbreaking thing this afternoon to get a chance to see him." She laughed. "What is it about that guy?"

"He's hot," offered the woman in the back.

"He's loaded," Mike added.

"And he's…" Liza looked at the paper right before she relinquished it to the checker to ring it in. "In *love*." And so, according to her insanely wild heartbeat, was she.

Laughing, the checker took the paper and squinted at the picture. "Let me read that. 'Despite the Ivory Glass billions,'" she read in a newscaster tone, "'Nate says the only family that matters to him is the one in his future with a lady he calls a wonder woman.'" She gave an exaggerated eye roll. "Gag me with the cheese, please."

"I think it's romantic," said the lady in back.

"I think—"

Liza whipped around and stopped whatever joke Mike was going to make. "You'd be wrong. And so would you," she said to the checker. Then she pointed to the woman behind him. "But you're right. He's romantic and hot. And I"—she gave an apologetic look to the cashier—"don't have time to pay for this."

They stared at her, shocked, but she didn't wait around, pushing the cart fast enough to get a gleeful shriek from Dylan. "Aunt Liza! Where are we going?"

"To your daddy," she whispered, scooping him out of the cart. "And we aren't going to almost-quite-not make it there in time."

The crowd around the patch of dirt in the central part of Barefoot Bay was sizable but still full of familiar faces to Nate. Zeke and Mandy stood arm in arm while the mayor made a speech. Becker and Frankie held hands, sharing jokes and teasing looks next to him. Several of the resort staff and townspeople had joined in and, of course, there was Julia Simpson, the reporter from *The Mimosa Times* who'd done such an incredible job with his story, and lots of folks from the local political scene.

But no Liza Lemanski.

After a few minutes, Nate stopped looking and concentrated on his job, which was to keep this little event rolling. He handed the mayor some facts and figures he'd been drawing up for the past week. He provided remarks for the local architect, too, but Clay Walker Jr., who'd also designed Casa Blanca Resort & Spa, spoke extemporaneously about the new project.

As Clay neared the end of his brief speech, Nate mentally checked off what came next, then opened his file for the list of county commissioners' names to thank. Flipping the papers, he didn't see the list. He knew it was in here. He straightened the folder and examined the papers again. Had he forgotten that? Once more, he looked, sensing he had about five seconds before Clay finished and he had to—

"It's right here." Two slender fingers reached into the file folder and slid out the list of names. "I put it right behind the commissioner's letter."

Nate snagged those fingers, squeezing as if they— and their owner—might disappear in a flash of his imagination. But she didn't. Instead, two beautiful blue-green eyes looked up at him, smiling, shining, and incredibly...*real*.

"Liza." He barely breathed the name he'd thought so many times in the last few weeks it felt like the four letters had been tattooed on his heart.

"I read the tabloids," she whispered as if she knew the hundred questions in his head. "You really need to be careful what you say to the media."

A slow smile curled his lips, a smile he felt it all the way down to his gut. "I told the truth."

"You're in love?"

Around him, the world faded away. The sights and sounds and worries evaporated as he gave his entire focus to the one thing that mattered. Could he tell her right here and now?

Could he *not*?

Somewhere, a throat cleared. A woman said, "Aww." And Becker snorted.

Only then did Nate look up and realize that Clay had stopped speaking, and everyone gathered around the soft dirt and oversized groundbreaking shovel was staring at him.

Nate pulled the list the rest of the way out of the folder and turned to Zeke. "Could you read this list and recognize these people? I'm kind of busy right now."

Zeke smiled and walked to the center of the ceremony while Nate closed his eyes with a soft laugh. "Yes," he finally answered her question. "I'm in love."

Her eyes widened along with her mouth, opening to a sweet little O that he desperately wanted to kiss. "What about you, Wonder Woman?"

For a long time, she didn't answer, holding his gaze and letting the air between them crackle with expectation. "I am, too," she whispered.

He couldn't wait any longer. Pulling her into him, he kissed her mouth with all the pent-up certainty that had been in his heart since she drove off and left him shattered.

Huge applause broke out, along with plenty of hoots and hollers. "I have a feeling," he mouthed into the kiss, "that isn't for the county commissioners."

She laughed and folded into him, wrapping her arms around him while they listened to Zeke announce that it was time for the first shovel of dirt. Holding Liza's hand, Nate walked forward and picked up the gold-painted spade, cameras humming and snapping all around.

Holding the shovel over the dirt, he glanced around, then settled on the only face in the crowd that mattered to him—the woman at his side. "I've never been more happier to be part of a great team," he announced.

As he stuck the shovel in the soft dirt, another cheer rose as he tossed the dirt to the side, one voice louder than the rest.

"D-I-G! Dig, dig, dig!"

Dylan's little legs were flying, but Liza's mother had a good grip on him, holding him in the back of the crowd. Nate gestured him over. "C'mere, buddy!"

Paulette let him go, and Dylan shot through the crowd straight to Nate, falling in the soft dirt the minute he reached it. That caused another eruption of crowd noise and cameras snapping, but all Nate saw was the beautiful face of his child.

Without thinking, he dropped to his knees, and Dylan reached up and threw filthy hands all over him, smearing his white Polo with dirt.

"Dylan!" Liza laughed, kneeling next to both of them.

"N-A-T-E!" he cried, smacking his hands on Nate's chest, making him howl with laughter.

"You know what I have to teach you, kid?"

"Not to rub dirt on nice white shirts?" Liza suggested.

He shook his head. "Another word to spell." He leaned closer to Dylan to whisper. "D-A-D."

Next to him, he heard Liza's sweet sigh of contentment, an echo of everything he felt right then. He put his arm around her and squeezed both of them with everything he had. "It'll go great with M-O-M."

Dylan threw a joyous handful of dirt into the air, letting it rain down all over the new Ivory family.

Yes, the billionaires have all found love, but there is a lot more romance ahead in Barefoot Bay. Here come the brides! Kick off your shoes and get to know some bridal consultants who've set up their destination wedding business on the shores of Barefoot Bay. While they're busy planning happily ever afters for their clients, they just might find one of their own!

Enjoy a sneak peek at

Barefoot in White,

The Barefoot Bay Series, Book 4.

"This one…" Willow sniffed her phone. "Yep, this one smells…" She sucked in a breath so deep it quivered her nostrils. "…like a whole bunch of trouble."

"Her texts stink?" Gussie looked up from her place on the floor, where she sat surrounded by about a hundred different swatches of fabric.

"Like Limburger in the sun." Willow exhaled and scrolled through the last five messages from the high-maintenance bride-to-be, clearing her throat to imitate this ass-pain of a bride. "My MOH and I will arrive at Casa Blanca on the fourth to do a full resort inspection and interview the wedding planning team, please include all amenities, especially all spa treatments."

"So, no groom?" Gussie asked with a derisive snort. "Just the bride and maid of honor to do a resort review and planning session? Sounds like an excuse for a girls' weekend of pampering and freebies, then they'll probably end up holding the wedding at a different resort."

"I doubt she'll find a place that fast." Willow kept reading. "Oh, this is my personal favorite. 'Our villa must have two bedrooms and baths with direct ocean view.'" She rolled her eyes. "Can she not read a map of Florida to see that Barefoot Bay is on the Gulf of Mexico, not the Atlantic Ocean?"

"I don't know if she can read a map, but I can tell you from the swatches she sent, she's color-blind." She waved some flesh-toned material.

"Oh, yeah. How are you doing with her 'all tones of sand' color palette selections?"

Gussie lifted a section of pale lace, the material barely covering the purple bangs of today's colorful wig. "You call this a palette? I call it beige, a dull and dangerous state of mind."

"Told you. This…" She squinted at the bride's name again. "Misty Trew is trouble." Willow locked the screen and set the phone on her desk. "Not only does she come with no referral, but who chooses a destination resort a month before the wedding?"

"Someone pregnant," Gussie suggested.

"Or someone the last bridal consultant dropped."

"Or someone"—the third member of the Barefoot Brides wedding planning team popped into the office doorway, her whole face covered by a giant gift basket—"with a mongo budget who can get what they want." Ari inched the basket to the side, her midnight eyes and jet-black hair contrasting the cream-colored bow around the cellophane wrapping. "Which is why I made this over-the-top welcome basket. Any volunteers to take it over to their villa? Bride and maid arrive in a few hours."

Willow pushed back and stood. "I'll go. I need the exercise."

Ari choked softly. "Says the woman who ran two miles this morning."

"Should have done four," Willow said as she took the basket, eyeing the mouthwatering contents. "Especially if I knew I'd be left alone with this box of truffles." She caressed the cellophane, giving a playful gasp when her fingers found an open seam. "Ooh, easy access, too."

"As if you'd touch a truffle," Ari teased.

"I have my moments. And our bride-to-be has a long list of demands, er, requests she sent, so I better make sure Artemisia is fully stocked right down to the Rosa Regale champagne that is, and I quote, '*The only thing I can possibly drink.*'"

"Spike it with Prozac while you're over there," Gussie suggested.

Laughing, Willow gathered the basket to her chest and headed out of the Casa Blanca Resort & Spa administration area where Barefoot Brides had its one-office headquarters. The upscale resort hummed with the activity of a typical Friday morning, gearing up for a busy weekend in Barefoot Bay.

Outside, the sun was high enough to make the gulf—*not the ocean*—sparkle turquoise, the water laced with white froth on a picture-perfect late-April morning. Bright yellow umbrellas spilled over the sand like lemon drops in the sunshine.

Willow chose the shady red-brick path that cut through the resort and led to each of the private villas, all named for different North African flowers in keeping with the Moroccan-inspired architecture. With each tap of her feet on the walkway, she let herself slip deeper in love with this piece of paradise.

They had to make this work, no matter how many high-maintenance brides put them through the wringer. Pooling their individual wedding consultant businesses to form Barefoot Brides had been her idea. The three of them moving here to run destination weddings at Casa Blanca was not only a unique selling point for clients…it was the key to Willow's personal happiness.

And she was happy, she reminded herself, humming a little, as though that soundtrack would prove the very thought to be true. So very happy and healthy and three thousand miles from California. New woman, new life, new everything.

Happy, happy, happy. The humming might be a little over-the-top, though.

Instead, she inhaled the briny bay air, stopping at the wrought iron gate that opened to Artemisia. Positioned on a rise, and angled so that the patio and pool faced the Gulf of Mexico, this butter-yellow villa was one of Willow's favorites on the property. Setting the basket on the terra cotta steps that led up to the front door, she pulled her resort ID that doubled as a master key out of her pocket, unlocked the door, and scooped up the goodies to go inside.

The living area was darkened from sunshades on the windows, cool and quiet, with the welcoming aroma of sweet gardenias left by the Casa Blanca cleaning staff. Heading to the kitchen, Willow froze mid-step at the sound of…was that running water? No. A footstep? She listened for a minute, heard nothing, then—

"Will ya…will ya…be my girl?"

Singing. Someone was singing. Well, more like howling. Woefully off-key.

"Gotta know if it's real, gotta know it's forevah!"

Willow's heart dropped so hard and fast the basket almost went with it. Was this some kind of joke? *That song*? That crappy, tacky, mess of metal that…that *pretended* to be a love song and paid for college and cars and everything else she'd had?

No one at this whole resort, on this island, or, hell, in the whole state of Florida, except for Ari and Gussie, could possibly know—

"No foolin' around, for worse or for bettah!"

Son of a bitch, who'd found her out? Did Ari or Gussie tell someone that Willow's father was a rock 'n' roll household name? They'd *promised* not to.

Gripping the basket so tight she could crack the wicker, she marched into the hallway that separated the two bedrooms, calling out, "Excuse me!"

"Will ya…will ya…be my…"

"Hey!" She lowered the basket to peer over the top and…oh. *Oh*.

Back.

Ass.

Muscles.

Ink.

Ass again. It deserved a second look.

"*Girrrrl*!" Tanned, muscular arms whacked the air, and a dark head of wet hair shook, sending droplets all the way down to…oh, really, that rear end was the most beautiful thing she'd ever seen.

"Come and take it, don't ya fake it, we can make—"

She opened her mouth, but nothing came out. The words caught in her throat, lost as her gaze locked on the bare-naked man air-drumming like a raving lunatic in the middle of the bedroom, totally unaware she stood behind him.

"Luh-uuuuve…" He destroyed the note, and not in the good way her father intended when he wrote the song. No, Donny Zatarain would probably weep if he heard his signature rock anthem being butchered by this idiot wearing nothing but noise-canceling headphones.

"Excuse me!"

His arms never missed a beat of the drum solo she had memorized before she was five years old, each stroke tensing and bulging muscles she hadn't even known existed. She opened her mouth to call out again, but that was a waste of time. Anyway, this particular feast for the eyes was way too good to pass up.

"Will ya, will ya be my *girrrrl*?"

But that song *had* to stop. She reached into the basket and grabbed the first thing her fingers touched: a nice ripe Florida orange. Yanking it out, she lobbed it as he hit the high C on "girl," except he didn't come anywhere near C, and the orange didn't go anywhere near him.

Still, he spun around, jumping into a wide, threatening stance, both arms out like a warrior ready to attack. She blocked her face with the basket, peeking through the top spray of cellophane, silently thanking Ari for choosing clear.

Whoa, that was a big…man.

"What the…" he muttered after a second, whipping off the headset. "I didn't hear you come in. You can put that down out there. Thanks."

She didn't move. Not even her eyes, which were riveted to…his…his…him.

"Thanks," he repeated, the word tinged with impatience. "You can leave now."

What if her client had come face-to-face with this? With that exposed…giant…breathtaking… She'd think this took "welcome package" to a whole new level.

"No, *you* can leave, because you are not in the right villa," she said.

He scowled. Well, she assumed he scowled. It was difficult to see his face because she couldn't stop looking at the rest of him.

"I'm in the right villa. Isn't this Art..Arte…some flower that starts with an A?"

Was she in the wrong place? No, of course not.

Get a grip, Willow. He was just a naked man—okay, an exceptionally stunning naked man—and she had a job to do here. Which was to get him out of the villa.

"Artemisia," she supplied, her arms starting to burn from holding the basket high enough to cover her face but still see. "And, yes, you *are* in the wrong villa, because we have guests booked to arrive soon, and you're not one of them."

He turned his hands skyward in a less threatening gesture, not that his hotter-than-a-thousand-suns body wasn't threatening enough. "Yes, I am," he said. "And if you will please turn around, miss, and leave that in the living room, we're cool."

"No, we are not cool." There was an understatement. "Because I'm pretty sure you have more, um, body hair than the bride or maid of honor we're expecting."

He took a step closer, and she hoisted the basket high enough to completely cover her face.

"Man," he said

"Excuse me?"

"I'm a man." With two hands, he lowered the basket. "As you've obviously noticed. *Man* of honor. Not *maid*."

The words registered, but not the meaning, because she was face-to-face with his broad chest and wide shoulders and a deep-purple tattoo of...oh, really? Was this God's idea of a joke? That was the earth and star on the cover of *Zenith*, the number-one best-selling Z-Train record of all time. "Really?"

"Really. I'm the man of honor in Misty Trew's wedding." His tone was a mix of waning tolerance and growing amusement.

She finally lifted her eyes, finally coherent enough to process what he'd said, and realize the mistake was hers. "I get it," she whispered, meeting cocoa-colored eyes as rich and inviting as the truffles in her arms, and a mouth that could be forgiven for whatever sour notes he'd hit with it, and...

Once more, the world slipped out from under her, this time because recognition nearly buckled her knees. "You're..." Her throat closed.

"The man of honor."

"No, you're..." The one who...the boy who...no, now the man who...crushed her spirit.

"A male version of the maid."

"You're..." Nick Hershey.

"Naked," he supplied, adding a slow, sexy, sinful smile. "But you're not."

She clung to the basket as if it were the last logical thing on earth because right now, it was. "I'm not..." How long had it been? Ten or eleven years since she'd

172

lived in a dorm at UCLA? And he'd been right down the hall. "Thinking straight."

"Clearly." He laughed and reached for the basket. "Here, let me take your junk so you can stop staring at mine." Placing the basket on the dresser, he held up a hand. "Just a sec. I'll get your tip."

"No tip, I'm not with the resort." The rote answer fell out of her mouth as he took a few steps, forcing Willow to stare some more at that round, hard handful of Nick Hershey's world-class ass before he disappeared into the en suite. "That ought to be illegal," she murmured on a sigh.

"So should breaking into a hotel room," he replied.

"I wasn't expecting…anyone. Or at least, not a man." Buck-naked. And she sure as hell hadn't been expecting the guy she'd tried to give her virginity to one slightly tipsy night after finals. *Tried* being the operative word, because he…

A dose of shame and a splash of self-pity mixed into a cocktail of humiliation, rising up to choke her. He'd turned her down cold and flat.

Willow rooted for a coherent thought, trying to center on the present. The bride was from New York. Nick was from California. How was it even possible that he was standing here in Mimosa Key, Florida?

It didn't matter. He was here, and a key member of the wedding party she was coordinating, so Willow would have to maintain professionalism and get control. She closed her eyes, willing her body and brain to get in line, the way she always did when she wanted to be stronger than whatever temptation or distraction threatened her well-honed control.

"So, you're a friend of Misty's?" she asked.

"Not exactly. Her brother is supposed to be here, but he's still deployed." He stepped back into the room, a towel wrapped around his hips, tied low, exposing a trail of dark hair that ran from his belly button down to his...no, no one could ever call what she'd just seen *junk*. "I'm doing him a favor and acting as Misty's second-in-command."

"She doesn't have a girlfriend to be the maid of honor?"

His brow quirked. "Have you met Misty?" he asked.

"No, not yet."

"Well, you'll understand when you see her. She's a model," he said, like that explained it. And, having been raised by one, it kind of did. "She's not exactly swimming in female companionship."

He crossed his arms and took another long, slow look at her, his gaze leaving a trail of heat, followed by goosebumps, and more heat. Still not even the slightest shadow of recognition. No surprise there.

Very few—actually none—of the people who knew her in college would recognize Willow Ambrose as Willie Zatarain. Not even someone who'd always said hello and made a point of being kind to her...but not *that* kind. Not kind or even drunk enough to sleep with a woman who outweighed him by more than a hundred pounds.

That was then, and this was...getting awkward.

"You know," he said, as if suddenly aware of how much time had passed while they looked at each other. "In the military, there's a rule that once you've seen someone naked, they get to see you naked."

Suddenly, a flash came back to her. Nick, friendly and even flirtatious when they were in college. His voice—at least when he wasn't singing—still had that smooth, silky quality that poured over her like hot fudge on cold ice cream. And like sundaes, he'd always been a temptation.

But Willow had long ago learned how to conquer temptations, hadn't she? "Good thing I'm not in the military, then. I get a pass."

The vaguest hint of disappointment darkened his eyes, giving her a surprising jolt of satisfaction. "Hey, can't blame a guy for trying. Lieutenant Nick Hershey." He extended his hand for a shake. "You don't work for the hotel, so are you one of the planner girls?"

"The planner girls?" She coughed a soft laugh, mostly to cover the certainty that he didn't remember her. The question was, should she refresh his memory? See the look of utter and abject shock on his face? Endure the questions, the litany of congratulations, and the embarrassment for both of them?

"Sorry, that sounded demeaning as shit, didn't it? I meant are you working for Misty as her wedding consultant?"

"Yes." She finally lifted her hand to slide into his, fighting a shudder when his warm, large fingers closed over hers.

"And you're..." he prompted.

"I'm..." *A girl you knew a long time ago.* Not that she could blame him. Most days, she didn't recognize herself. "Willow Ambrose."

"Willow." He let the word roll around on his lips, tasting it, nodding as if he liked it a lot, smiling as though meeting her for the first time. Well, wasn't that why she'd ditched the shortened nickname and lopped off her world-famous last name?

"The pleasure is...well, I guess the initial pleasure was yours." He winked, and it hit her heart like a red-hot spark.

"Not the singing part," she teased.

He laughed, a low rumble in his chest that she *knew* could curl toes, melt hearts, and vacuum up phone numbers. "I suck, I know. But that's how I relax. Does your job mean I'll be seeing a lot of you this weekend?" The little bit of hope in his voice tweaked her heart, still not grasping the fact that *he* was flirting with *her*.

"Depends on how much wedding planning you and the BTB are going to do."

"BTB? Wait, don't tell me. Bride That Bitches?"

It was her turn to laugh. "Bride To Be, but your version is often dead-on, too. I thought you and Misty weren't going to be here for a few hours."

"We came from different places, and I got bumped to an earlier flight, and she's...somewhere." He put his hands on his narrow hips, the move accentuating his chest and pecs and stunningly cut abs. "Want to show me around until she gets here?"

Could she...not tell him? The thought landed in her head with a thud. It would be dishonest not to tell him they'd known each other a dozen years...and a hundred and twenty pounds ago.

Except, he'd known Willie Zatarain, the fat girl in Sproul Hall who had few friends and famous parents. He didn't know Willow Ambrose. And by the way he was looking at her, he wanted to.

The powerful, dizzying, irresistible pull of temptation tugged at her insides. This time, just this one time, temptation kicked her ass.

"Yes," she said softly. "I'll show you around."

Don't Miss a Moment in Barefoot Bay!

Don't miss Roxanne St. Claire's latest popular series, The Dogfather, which is chock full of hot guys, cute dogs, true love...and one great big Irish family you will adore!

Daniel Kilcannon is known as "The Dogfather" for a reason. It's not just his renowned skills as a veterinarian, his tremendous love of dogs, or the fact that he has turned his homestead in the foothills of the Blue Ridge Mountains into a world class dog training and rescue facility. Ask his six grown children who run Waterford Farm for him, and they'll tell you that their father's nickname is due to his uncanny ability to pull a few strings to get what he wants. And what he wants is for his four sons and two daughters to find the kind of life-changing love he had with his dearly departed wife, Annie. This old dog has a few new tricks...and he'll use them all to see his pack all settled into their happily ever afters!

Every book in the Dogfather series features a rescue dog on the cover and a portion of proceeds are donated to the Alaqua Animal Refuge, where the covers were photographed. And every story has a dog at the heart of the romance...front, center, and sometimes right in between. If you love dogs and romance, this series is for you!

THE DOGFATHER SERIES

About The Author

Published since 2003, Roxanne St. Claire is a *New York Times* and *USA Today* bestselling author of more than fifty romance and suspense novels.

In addition to being an ten-time nominee and one-time winner of the prestigious RITA™ Award for the best in romance writing, Roxanne's novels have won the National Readers' Choice Award for best romantic suspense four times, as well as the Maggie, the Daphne du Maurier Award, the HOLT Medallion, Booksellers' Best, Book Buyers Best, the Award of Excellence, and many others.

A recent empty-nester, she lives in Florida with her husband, and still attempts to run the lives of her young adult children. She loves dogs, books, chocolate, and wine, especially all at the same time!

www.roxannestclaire.com
www.twitter.com/roxannestclaire
www.facebook.com/roxannestclaire
www.instagram.com/roxannestclaire1

Made in the USA
Monee, IL
04 July 2020